THE TRAIL TO RESTORATION

PLAINSMAN WESTERN SERIES BOOK THREE

B.N. RUNDELL

WOLFPACK PUBLISHING
— EST 2013 —

The Trail to Restoration
Print Edition
© Copyright 2022 B.N. Rundell

Wolfpack Publishing
5130 S. Fort Apache Rd. 215-380
Las Vegas, NV 89148

wolfpackpublishing.com

Paperback ISBN 978-1-63977-004-5
Ebook ISBN 978-1-63977-005-2
LCCN 2021950018

THE TRAIL TO RESTORATION

This book has been a little more difficult than the others, but only because we, both my wife and I, were stricken with the Covid 19. It was a challenging time, but the good Lord saw us through, and we are looking forward to many more rides with our readers. I am grateful to our family, and I dedicate this to the two daughters, Kerri Farmer from Michigan, and Kacee Rundell from Wyoming, that came to our side and nursed us through the plague from China! They left their families to come to our aid and we might not have made it without them. Thanks girls! You're the best!

"My father, Little Owl, went to Fort Laramie to sign the treaty two hands and two years ago. We were promised all the land from the North Platte River to the Arkansas River, and from the mountains to the land of the Smoky Hill River. But the soldiers of Fort Laramie soon broke that treaty. I made peace with the Cheyenne, Comanche, Kiowa, and Apache. Chief Niwot went with me to meet with the men that dig for yellow stone in the mountains of the great peak, there," pointing to the southwest to reference Pikes Peak, "and we made peace with the white men.

"The leaders of those white men came again, asked us to Fort Wise to sign another treaty to take away what they said was ours. Black Kettle of the Cheyenne and five," holding up his hand with all fingers extended, "of his chiefs, and Big Mouth, Storm, Shave-Head, and," tapping his chest, "Little Raven, signed to bring peace by giving away much of our land. Now they say our land is only far south of here. But my people and the Cheyenne Dog Soldiers do not agree. The white men that signed said there would be no more white men

1

come onto our lands, but they lie. I believe war between the whites and our people will come soon." Little Raven dropped his gaze to the smoldering embers of the morning cookfire. "We followed the herds of buffalo north for the hunt, but the white men say we are away from our lands. We will return south when we are ready." They sat beside the tipi provided by Little Raven and his people for Reuben and his new bride, Elly. But the week of being alone after their joining was over and the Arapaho had returned for the hide lodge.

Reuben looked at his friend, Little Raven, the chief of the *Hinono'eino*, the Arapaho people who had befriended him just recently during a buffalo hunt and a meeting with two wagon trains. The chief and his people had helped prepare Reuben Grundy and his bride, Eleanor Ann McGuire, 'Elly', for their joining ceremony and had celebrated with them. Now the time had come to part ways, and they were saying their farewells.

"I'm saddened to hear that, Little Raven. You have done much to bring peace between our people and if there is war between our people, many will die," replied Reuben, looking at his friend's saddened countenance.

"I am to go to the village of the great white father in Washington. Perhaps I will talk him into peace between our people."

Reuben smiled, nodding, "I hope you do, Little Raven. But President Lincoln has much on his mind, especially the war between the North and the South."

"Why do your people fight one another?"

Reuben shook his head, "I suppose it is much like the natives of this land. The Pawnee fight the Osage, the Sioux fight the Otoe, the Crow fight the Sioux, and on and on, just like the many different people of the east, the Union fights the Confederacy, the Bushwhackers fight the Red Legs, and more."

"They should be like us," offered Little Raven, motioning to himself and Reuben, "We are different, but we can agree on peace and be friends."

Reuben smiled as he stood, "I agree, Little Raven, and you have been a good friend. But Yellow Bird," thinking of the name given his woman by the Arapaho women, "and I must be on our way."

Little Raven reached out to clasp forearms with the chief and the big man drew him close, "We must always be friends. Whenever you meet other Arapaho, tell them you are a friend to *Hosa*, Little Raven, and you will be treated as a friend."

Elly was outside by their horses, admiring the gift from her friends, Running Antelope and Wind in her Hair, the two women that had made her wedding tunic. She stood beside a leopard Appaloosa mare with a beautiful Indian saddle with a tall pommel and high cantle, white buckskin across the seat and covering the girth and stirrup leathers. The soft-eyed mare stood stock still, letting Elly stroke her neck and talk to her. She had been assured the horse was a spirited but well-trained animal and she was excited about the beauty of the mare. She looked to Reuben, "Isn't she beautiful?"

"She is that." He looked to the women, now standing beside the first wife of Little Raven, Red Bear, and using sign and English, knowing Red Bear understood, he thanked the women and Little Raven for the gift of the horse.

"Every time I ride her, I will think of you," declared Elly, looking from one to the other of her new friends. "I am so grateful, and I hope we will see you again!" she added, as she made a little hop, stuffed her foot in the stirrup and swung her leg over the high cantle. She wore buckskin leggings under the long, beaded tunic that the women made for her. It was similar in style to the wedding tunic, but not as elaborate and of a darker shade of gold.

Reuben mounted his blue roan, snatched up the lead to the pack mule, and with a wave and a nod, led them away from their honeymoon lodge to start the first leg of their journey to the south. They were bound for Julesburg, the stage station that was rapidly becoming a village and was where they hoped to begin their new life together.

Little Raven had given Reuben directions for their journey to Julesburg, "Follow the creek we call Rush Creek south. When it turns west, you leave the creek. Look to the south and east to the sand hills. The trail is faint, but the sign of our passing will show. Follow that trail to another creek, two days south. That is the Lodgepole Creek and will join the South Platte River. Downstream is Julesburg."

It was mid-day when they came to the bend in the creek that marked the point where they would take to the sand hills, and Reuben shaded his eyes, looked at the inviting creek and the cottonwoods offering shade. "That," pointing with his chin to the shade, "is more inviting than that," nodding to the dry sand hills and the vista of cacti, sage, and scattered piñon.

"I agree, and I am getting a little hungry," smiled Elly with a bit of a giggle. "What'chu fixing?"

"Now listen here, woman. We need to get somethin' straight. I shoot 'em, you cook 'em."

She laughed again, "So, if I shoot 'em, you'll cook 'em?"

"Well, we'll talk about that later," he responded with a

crooked smile painting his face. He swung down, stepped beside her, and offered his hands to help her to the ground. He looked at the saddle and said, "Is that thing comfortable? It looks like a torture rack."

She laughed, glancing back at the saddle, "Well, it sure is pretty, but no, it's not real comfortable. But I think it's better than riding bareback."

Reuben took the reins of the appaloosa together with those of Blue and the mule to lead them to the creek for water. Elly started gathering some dry wood for a small fire and in short order, the animals were picketed, girths loosened, and they were enjoying the spring grasses, and a small fire was flaring with the coffeepot sitting close.

"So, how far have we come?" asked Elly, spearing some strips of fresh meat on the willow withes to hang over the flames.

"Oh, maybe eight or ten miles. We'll rest up a spell, let the horses get some feed and rest, then we'll get another ten or so 'fore we stop for the night."

"Didn't Little Raven say that Julesburg was about three days' ride?"

"Ummhmm, but we're in no hurry. We'll not push it. When we get there, we get there."

"I like how you think. It seems like on the wagon train it was hurry, hurry, hurry. We had to travel as far and as fast as we could every day. It was so tiring, especially when we had to walk all the time to save the oxen." She shook her head at the memory, thinking of her family still on the westward trek. She smiled as she looked up at Reuben. "You think you can get on with the stage line?"

"Prob'ly. The driver I talked to said they were always lookin' for help."

"Why?"

"Why what?"

"Why are they always looking for help?"

"I dunno, guess men come and go. Maybe some light out for the gold fields, others just get tired of bouncin' on the stages all the time, and he did say there were robberies whenever the gold is shipped, and sometimes attacks by Indians."

"I thought Little Raven said there was a peace treaty."

"He did. But the last two treaties he signed; the whites broke 'em. And he says many of the young braves of the Arapaho and the Cheyenne aren't too happy about the treaty. It takes away a lot of their land, takes away the buffalo huntin' grounds. For that matter, where Little Raven's band was huntin', was off the treaty lands."

Sudden movement caught Reuben's attention and he looked at Blue, his blue roan gelding, who had lifted his head quickly and stood with head high, ears pricked and nostrils flaring. Reuben stood and turned to look and saw riders coming from the sand hills toward them. He glanced back at the fire, noting Elly had properly built a small fire, dry wood, little smoke and under the wide spreading branches of a sycamore. Any smoke would be dissipated by the branches and the line of chokecherry bushes and willows shielded them from view.

He slowly moved to the saddlebags to retrieve his binoculars and stood in the shade of the cottonwood as he lifted the field glasses for a view of the riders. Elly had come to his side and whispered, "Who are they?"

"Dunno. They're not Arapaho, maybe the Cheyenne Dog Soldiers that Little Bear mentioned." He kept his eyes on the group, counted fourteen riders, and watched as they came from the low swale between two low hills. "They're not painted, trailin' some pack horses, prob'ly just a huntin' party. But..." he let the comment hang between them as he considered what he saw. He watched as they moved, trying to guess where they were bound and if the band would come closer to them. The two men at the head of the band rode side by side and were impressive figures. Both had sashes across their chests and Reuben remembered Little Raven telling of Dog soldiers, so called because of a dog rope, a hide or hair rope they wore as a sash over one shoulder and across their chest to their opposite side at the waist. They would stake the rope into the ground, and fight the battle without removing the rope, bound to the stake to fight where they were. They were considered the fiercest of all warriors. As they neared, he also saw two women among them, but both were bound and gagged, riding in front of a warrior with his arms on either side.

"I think they just came from a raid. Looks like they've got a couple captive women."

"Let me see!" demanded Elly, reaching for the binoculars. Reuben lowered the field glasses, and begrudgingly handed them to her.

"Stay back in the shade so the sun doesn't give you away," cautioned Reuben.

He heard the low gasp that came from Elly, as she watched the band draw nearer. She lowered the binoculars, looking to Reuben, "We've got to do something!" she declared, giving Reuben a pleading look that reminded him of when he rescued her and her friends from the Sioux.

He shook his head, reaching for the binoculars, and lifted them to his eyes. "There's a dozen warriors with those two women!"

"So?" she asked, her voice imploring with an unrealistic expectation.

"But the Cheyenne are friends with the Arapaho!" muttered Reuben, still watching the warriors.

"So? Those women are scared to death! We have to help them somehow!" she demanded.

"You're not goin' to let this go, are you?" he retorted, lowering the glasses to look at her.

"If that was me, you'd find some way to help, wouldn't you?"

"Yeah, but it's not you. But if we try somethin', if might end up bein' you and me!"

Elly shook her head, touching his arm and looking up at him. "Please?"

R euben rode from the small clearing, leading the
pack mule, and moved into the open before the
tree line. The leader of the Cheyenne raised a hand to
stop his warriors while still about fifty yards from the
creek. Cocking his head slightly to the side, he watched
the white man as he sat his horse, looking toward the
raiding party of Cheyenne. The leader, Tall Bull, chief of
the Dog Soldiers of the Cheyenne, spoke softly to the
warrior beside him, "What is this white man doing?"

Lone Bear responded, "Maybe he wants to trade?"
pointing at the pack mule with his chin.

The warrior behind Tall Bull offered, "I will go see
this man. Do we trade or kill him and take his goods?"

"You choose, Pile of Bones," ordered the chief. The
band of twelve had been on a raid of the ranches along
the South Platte and were returning to their encampment in Nebraska territory beyond the North Platte
River. Although Black Kettle and other chiefs of the
Cheyenne had signed the Treaty of Fort Wise that gave
much of their land back to the whites, Tall Bull and his
Dog Soldiers had refused to join the others. They were

determined to keep their lands where the great herds of buffalo could be hunted, and they would fight against the many whites that wanted to settle on this land. But Tall Bull was smart enough to know a fight against the white men and their many rifles and other weapons would soon be lost unless they could steal and trade for such weapons. Although he had captured a white man and taken his pistol, the rifle had been shattered in the fight, but a pistol was nothing compared to the far shooting rifles which he coveted. The warriors watched as Pile of Bones, the warrior chosen by Tall Bull to go to the white man, approached the buckskin attired man.

Reuben sat silent as he watched the lone rider draw near and lifted his hand high, palm forward as he greeted the man in Arapaho, "Heebee," then using sign he explained, "I come to trade. I have goods," motioning to the packs on the mule. "I am a friend of Little Raven of the Arapaho and have traded with his people."

The rider sat stone faced as he watched Reuben use sign. His expression showed some surprise when he mentioned Little Raven, and the man moved closer, looking at Reuben with a skeptical eye. Reuben noticed the warrior had a flint-lock pistol in his belt and proudly carried a trade fusil rifle across the withers of his mount. He also noticed the hammer was cocked on the rifle and the man's finger was on the trigger, but the muzzle was pointed away. The warrior balanced the rifle across his thighs and the withers of the horse as he used both hands to sign to Reuben. "We will talk trade, lay your goods out in the grass by the creek," nodding to the clearing where Reuben and Elly had stopped for their nooning. The warrior reined around and started back to the others, glancing over his shoulder at Reuben to see if he was going back into the clearing.

Reuben reined Blue around, jerked on the lead of the mule and spoke just loud enough for Elly to hear. "We're comin' back to the clearin'. Take your horse into the trees, but keep your rifle handy and stay under cover, but watch the trade, just in case." He hoped she heard and moved quickly away before the Cheyenne followed him into the shady area. Fearful of what the many warriors would do at the sight of Elly, he wanted her away and out of danger, but he was also apprehensive of the Cheyenne. Little Raven had spoken of the Dog Soldiers, saying they were the most fearsome fighters in the territory.

Relieved that she had vacated the clearing, Reuben quickly stripped the packs and gear from the mule, ground tied his blue roan, and glanced to the thicket as he heard the whispers of Elly, "I'm watching you!"

He chuckled and answered, "Just stay out of sight!"

The blanket spread, he lay out the knives, hatchets, and other trade goods, although his supply was considerably depleted. What he had received in return from the Arapaho would be of little use to the Cheyenne, but he did lay out a few items, beaded necklaces, the hair-pipe bone necklace from Little Raven with the nuggets removed, and a few pelts of otter and beaver. He stood back away from the goods, near his roan, and watched as the leader and three of his men walked into the clearing. The others were beyond the line of berry bushes, apparently making a camp for a meal, while several led their horses to water at the creek. Reuben knew Elly was behind him, and hoped she remained still and out of sight.

The chief walked to the blanket, looked at the goods, glanced up at Reuben and spoke in English, "Pile of

Bones," motioning to the first warrior, "said you are a friend of Little Raven."

"My name is Reuben. Yes, I am a friend of Little Raven. He and his people were on a hunt by the North Platte. We traded and visited."

"Little Raven is a little man," stated the chief, casually looking at the goods on the blanket.

"No, he is a big man," and Reuben used his hands to indicate the height and breadth of the big chief, "taller and broader than I am." Reuben suspected the chief was testing him.

The chief nodded, "I am Tall Bull, chief of the Dog Soldiers of the *Tsêhéstáno*, or Cheyenne people." He paused as he looked from the trade goods back to Reuben, "You have nothing I want. I look for rifles and pistols to hunt the buffalo. Do you have rifles?"

"What would you trade for a rifle?" asked Reuben, "I do not see anything I want," looking from Tall Bull to the others that were touching and examining the knives and hatchets and more.

"What would you want for a rifle?" asked Tall Bull, trying to casually look around the camp for any rifles that Reuben might have, but Reuben had slipped the Sharps out of the scabbard and stood it behind the trunk of the sycamore.

"I see you have two white women. Perhaps I would take the women, two horses, and your breast plate," nodding toward the hair-pipe bone breast plate that hung over the broad chest of the chief.

"What rifle to you have? You ask for much and it is probably like that old rifle of Lone Bear," pointing to one of the warriors that stood by the blanket, a rifle standing beside him as he examined a hatchet.

"It is a far shooting rifle. A buffalo rifle that can kill a buffalo from far away."

The chief's eyes flared, and he lifted his head slightly, looking down his nose at Reuben. The two men were of the same height and similar stature. Tall Bull had his thick hair parted in the middle, wore three feathers at the back of his head, and had long braids with tufts of fur woven into the braids. A hair-pipe bone breastplate with beads and leather separators covered his broad chest and his beaded and fringed leggings, with scalps tied with the fringe, sided a breech cloth that hung to his knees and showed a diamond within a diamond beaded pattern that matched the beads on his moccasins. A wide carved silver band encircled his upper arm, accenting the bulging biceps. His manner was intimidating, but a touch of mischievousness glinted from his eyes and tugged at the corners of his mouth.

Reuben thought, *this man thinks he's playing with me, he's up to something and I'm guessing that something is no good.*

"I would see this rifle."

"When I see the women. If they are old and fat, you will have to add something to the trade," declared Reuben, somberly.

The chief let a grin show, nodded, and motioned to Pile of Bones, the skinny warrior that suited his name, and sent him after the captives.

The women were frightened, their tear-streaked faces showed bruises and scratches where they had probably fought their captors, and their clothing was tattered, dirty, and torn, appearing as nothing more than rags. One of the women, the slightly older of the two, was a brown-haired hellion that fought and pushed back with every move she made. Her eyes showed anger and determination, but their mouths were stuffed with rags and the only sound was a muffled plea. But the mutters from the first woman left little to the imagination, undoubtedly filled with threats and pleas. The warrior pushed her forward and she stumbled and fell, catching herself with her bound hands, and turned and snarled at the warrior as she stood, kicking sand at him.

The second woman was more docile, tears still making paths through the dirt on her cheeks, her head hung in dejected resignation, and she showed no resistance to the shoving of the warrior as he moved her closer. Her hair was a dark auburn, her eyes green, her face was fair complected with freckles galore, but her spirit had been stifled. She did not look at anything but her own feet, fearful of showing any resistance for fear of a beating.

The chief had noticed the pattern of beads on the buckskins worn by Reuben, recognizing it as Arapaho, and had become a little more accepting of the white man trader. But he was more interested in the rifle Reuben had spoken of and now said, "I would see the rifle."

Reuben acted as if he had not heard the man and walked close to the women, lifting the chin of the hellion, and looking into her defiant eyes. She mumbled something that sounded like a threat and Reuben chuckled, looked at the chief and said, "This one is like a wild she-bear!" and as the chief chuckled, moved to the second woman. A cursory examination had shown there were no serious injuries to either woman. He turned back to the chief, "I dunno, Tall Bull, but I'll show you the rifle."

As he lifted the rifle from behind the sycamore, he hefted it to his side and walked back to show the chief. He was not happy with the possible trade, never wanting to give any weapon to anyone that might turn them against the settlers and others, but he had little else to trade and there were definitely too many to fight. He handed the rifle to the chief and stepped back as he examined the weapon.

"You said this is a shoots far rifle. Show me," and handed it back to Reuben.

Reuben nodded, accepting the rifle and dropped the lever to open the breech. He inserted a paper cartridge, closed the chamber, and placed a percussion cap on the nipple, readying the rifle to fire. He nodded to Tall Bull and motioned for him to follow as he walked from the clearing into the open beyond the line of berry bushes. He stopped, looking into the distance for a target and spotted a shoulder of rocks at the edge of a low hill about four hundred yards distant. He looked back at the chief, "That rock yonder, at the edge of the hill," pointing to the target.

The chief walked closer, frowning, and looking at the distant rock, and back at Reuben. "You will shoot that rock?" asked the chief, doubt showing in his expression.

"Ummhmm," replied Reuben, "And if I hit it, we have a trade, right?"

"One woman, one horse," replied the chief.

Reuben lowered the rifle, shaking his head, "No, two women, two horses, a strong bow and a full quiver of arrows."

"Two women, two horses, this rifle and two hatchets and two knives."

"Two women, two horses, for this rifle and one hatchet and one knife."

"It is good. But you hit rock first," declared the chief.

Reuben reached forth his hand to shake, and the chief complied. He looked at Reuben as he took a knee, lifted

15

the rifle with his left hand, resting his left elbow on his knee, and slowly took aim. With a slow squeeze, he tightened his grip on the front trigger and the rifle roared, bucked, and spat smoke, startling the chief who jumped back. He had been watching the rock and never took his eyes away, so that when the lead slug struck the sandstone, the rock crumpled, split, and fell from the pile. Reuben stood up, cradling the rifle in his arm, and smiled at Tall Bull.

"Satisfied?"

The chief stepped close and reached for the rifle, "It *is* a far shooting rifle!" he declared.

Reuben held tight. "The women?" as he looked at the chief.

Tall Bull turned toward Lone Bear who had followed them into the flats, "The women are his," and motioned him back to the clearing. Reuben handed the rifle to the chief, and they walked together back to the clearing. Some of the other warriors were anxious to barter for some hatchets and knives and the trades were quickly completed, and the entire band started away. Tall Bull clasped forearms with Reuben, "Reuben is a friend with Tall Bull and the Cheyenne."

"That is good, Tall Bull. I am honored to be a friend with you and your people. May we always meet together in peace."

The chief nodded, swung aboard his mount, and lay his new rifle across the withers of his white stallion, grinning down at Reuben. "Tell your friend in the woods he can come out now. We leave."

Reuben chuckled, nodded, and said, "That friend is my woman, Yellow Bird, and she had a rifle on you all the time."

The chief grinned, nodded, and led the band of

warriors away, moving downstream and to the north, bound for the North Platte and their encampment beyond. Reuben watched them leave and Elly came to his side, "Let's tend to the women."

When the women saw Elly, their eyes grew wide and watched as she removed their gags and bonds, each one hugging her as they tearfully thanked her and looked at Reuben to express their thanks.

"I am Sadie Slade, and this is Mabel Masengale. We were taken from our ranch down on the South Platte and we were afraid we would never live to see our home again. Thank you, thank you, thank you," pleaded the brown-haired woman, then her expression changed, "And what do you mean calling me a she-bear?!"

Reuben laughed, prompting the others to join in the laughter as he explained, "I was just tryin' to make a better deal. If I acted like I wanted you, he would have raised the price and Elly there was listenin' from the bushes, and I didn't want her to think wrong about me!" The women laughed again, not so much at the gaiety of the moment as the relief of the tension and fear.

17

3 / LODGEPOLE

T he women were hungry, having traveled for two days with the Cheyenne and never fed, their first thought once freed was for food. Elly took charge, giving Reuben directions, "You stir up the coals and hang some more meat, please," pausing to give him a broad smile of appreciation, "while we take care of cleaning up and making these ladies a bit more comfortable." Without waiting for a response, she led the two women to the paniers beside the mule, and with her arms laden, she nodded toward the creek for the two women to take a dip in the cool water.

Reuben tended to the fire, the meat, and a fresh pot of coffee for himself, while the women were frolicking in the creek beyond the thicket of cottonwoods. He shook his head, chuckling to himself. *Reckon that's the way with women. Get rescued from bloodthirsty Indians, and all they wanna do is take a bath.*

Elly had kept a few of her clothes from the wagon train and let the two women clothe themselves in the simple dresses. Both dresses were gingham, and Sadie, being about the same size as Elly, filled out the blue one.

But Mabel was a bit smaller, and Elly used a few pins on the green one to take in the slack so she would not feel uncomfortable. The women helped one another with their hair, and when the three walked back into the clearing, Reuben was caught off guard when Elly cleared her throat to get his attention, and he almost spilled the coffee. When he took in the sight before him, he was surprised in the change; even Elly had let her hair down and looked to be glowing in the afternoon light. The other two women were bashfully smiling, but pleased at Reuben's reaction, "Well, if I didn't know better, I'd think you were not the same women that we found just a while ago!"

Elly smiled and giggled, and she walked closer to her husband and took his arm as she turned back to look at the women. "They do look nice, don't they?"

"Ummhmm, and I've got the fixin's ready if everybody's hungry!"

The women quickly changed from bashful girls to famished women and wasted little time gathering up some sticks with sizzling meat strips and a cup of coffee. Reuben had baked some timpsila in the coals and dragged them out with a stick, rolled them onto a tin plate and peeled the skins off to reveal the pale flesh of the prairie turnips, and offered them to the ladies, who gladly accepted and soon devoured them.

They were soon on the trail south, bound for the Lodgepole creek that would lead them to Julesburg and back to the ranch where the girls had been taken. As they rode, Sadie explained, "We were riding on the upper end of the ranch when the Indians attacked. When we heard the fighting, we took off for the ranch, but the Indians caught us before we made it. The last we saw was smoke coming from the buildings, so we don't know if anyone survived the fight. It didn't last long, and all we saw that the Indians stole was not from our ranch. Mabel's father worked with my father at the ranch and our mothers were there, and I have a little sister too. Mabel has an older brother, and there were two other men that worked at the ranch."

"Where is your ranch?" asked Reuben.

"Between the Spring Hill station and Dennison's ranch, both are stage stops. But our ranch is on the other side of the river from the stage line."

"How long has the ranch been there?" asked Elly, riding beside Reuben, with Sadie and Mabel behind them.

"My father started the ranch three years ago when his brother came to Julesburg for the stage line. His brother, Jack Slade, has a ranch near the confluence of the North and South Platte, by Cottonwood Springs. He, my uncle Jack, was asked by Butterfield to come to Julesburg because of a problem with Jules Beni who had the stage station at the time. My father, Fritz, came out with him and started the ranch. That was almost four years ago."

"Did your uncle take care of the problem at the station?" asked Reuben, curious as to the history of the stage line.

Sadie laughed, "Boy, did he! Uncle Jack was known to be sort of a gunman, he taught me how to shoot, and the problem was Jules Beni, who started the first trading post, restaurant, bar, and more and the place is named after him, but he became an outlaw. He was stealing from the stage line, stealing horses from the ranchers and the line, and more. So he and Uncle Jack got into it and Beni shot my uncle four or five times, left him for dead and took off. But Uncle Jack didn't die and got better and vowed to even the score with Beni. But it took almost two years before Uncle Jack caught up with him, captured him, tied him to a fence post and shot off his fingers, then stuck the pistol in Beni's mouth and pulled the trigger!" She laughed at the memory and the many variations of the story that had been told. She continued, "Then he cut off his ears and kept them as trophies!"

Elly shook her head and said, "Some Uncle you've got!"

Sadie laughed, grew silent and quietly added, "Yeah, but he's gone now. He lost his wife in an Indian raid, took to drinking, and my family has been worried about him. He was fired by the stage line for drinking and left the country. Last we heard, he was up in Montana, they think he's turned plumb mean and bad."

They rode quiet for a while, moving through the dry sand hills, keeping to the low swales, and using the contours of the land for cover. This was the land of both the Arapaho and the Cheyenne and Reuben would not feel comfortable, being responsible for three women now, until they were in better country that offered more cover.

"The land beyond these hills is like a big mesa, flat land with grasses and more trees. Compared to the rest of the area, it's considered high country, but the soil is good, and my Pa says he thinks one day it'll be good farmland," explained Mabel.

"You think we'll make it to the Lodgepole creek 'fore dark?" asked Reuben, twisting around in his saddle to look back at the two women.

Sadie answered as she shaded her eyes to look at the sun, "Maybe. It'll be easier traveling when we're on the flats."

THE SUN WAS TUCKING ITSELF BEHIND THE LOW HORIZON off the right shoulder of the riders as they dropped into the dry gulch between the low sandhills. As they rounded the shoulder on their right, the shallow gulch with the sandy bottom pushed the hills away and showed a glimmer of green before them. Sadie pushed her mount forward beside Reuben, pointing to the line of green, "That's the Lodgepole! It ain't much of a creek, but it's good water and there's plenty of grass and trees."

"Where's your ranch from here?" inquired Reuben, standing in his stirrups to look into the opening valley.

"The Cheyenne took the hard way over the sand hills straight north from our ranch. It's a little further to follow the creek to the South Platte, then upstream to our ranch, but it's a better trail, plenty of water and cover. It's about a half day's ride from here."

"Then you won't mind if we make camp and get an early start?"

"No, of course not. I'm anxious to get home and see about my family, but I'm tired and I know the horses need rest. I can wait," answered Sadie, glancing back at Mabel who nodded in agreement.

"Good," replied Reuben as he turned to Elly. "I'll need to see if I can get us some fresh meat, so, if you can spare the Henry..." he started, holding out his hand for the rifle that Elly had commandeered and claimed as her own.

"Well, maybe you should make camp and start supper while I go hunting," she offered, a mischievous grin splitting her face.

"So, you wanna kill some helpless deer, split him open and reach into his bloody belly and pull out those guts and such, then load him up onto your horse and bring him back to camp, all by your lonesome?"

She laughed her giggly laugh and offered a coy smile

as she answered, "Oh, maybe not. I think I'll leave the blood and guts to you, for now anyway." She turned to look at the others, "You ladies think we can make camp while the great white hunter goes for fresh meat?"

"Can he be trusted out of our sight?" playfully asked Sadie.

"Oh, I s'pose," replied Elly, handing the Henry to Reuben.

WHEN REUBEN RETURNED, THE WOMEN HAD A DUTCH oven full of biscuits baking at fire's edge, some prairie turnips baking in the coals beside some fresh cattail shoots, and the coffeepot was dancing beside the fire, but the fire was obscured by Elly and Sadie who stood side by side, their backs to the fire as they watched Reuben step down from Blue.

"Where's the fresh meat?" asked Elly, bending side to side to look at the horse.

"Uh, weren't any," answered a dejected Reuben, unable to look at the women as he led the roan to water. He did not notice the girls moving as he walked, still obscuring the fire.

"Oh, well, I guess we'll just go hungry," declared Elly, trying to keep a straight face as she watched Reuben strip the gear from his roan.

"Don't we have some jerky and pemmican you can make a stew with?" he asked, glancing over his shoulder to see the women still standing close beside one another. He frowned at their antics, turned to face them. "Alright, what's up?"

"Oh, nothing," replied Elly. "But we thought you might come back empty handed so we tried to make do with what we could get, so wash up cuz' supper's ready!"

Reuben frowned, watching the girls move aside to reveal a roasting turkey on a spit over the fire, dripping juices into the flames and looking a sumptuous golden brown. His brow furrowed as he looked at the bird, then at the snickering women, and shook his head. "Alright, how'd you do that?"

"We saw it, and the three of us cornered it, and Sadie tackled it! Ain't it sumpin'?" asked Elly, smiling broadly and motioning to the dripping turkey.

"Ummhmm, and so are you! All of you!" declared a smiling and laughing Reuben as he walked to the fire.

4 / RIDERS

W ith an early start, they rode with the sun in their
face, until the Lodgepole creek made a bend to
the south and the sun rose higher. Sadie was anxious and
they hoped to make it to the Slade ranch by midday.
Reuben reined up, lifting his hand to stop the girls, and
stood in his stirrups as he shaded his eyes. Four riders
were coming toward them, and Reuben could tell they
had already been spotted as the men fanned out to stop
them. They were over three hundred yards apart and
Reuben told Elly, "Get your rifle ready, I'm not sure
about those riders. They're white men, but..."

He sat back in his saddle and lifted his Remington
Army revolver from its holster at his hip and held it
behind the pommel of his saddle out of sight. Sadie
pushed her mount beside Reuben and reached out to lift
his metal-bladed tomahawk from his belt. He glanced at
her as she smiled a wicked smile, shaking her head. "I
don't like being unarmed and I'm pretty handy with one
of these," she stated, keeping her eyes on the riders.

They waited for the men to draw near until Reuben
called out, "That's close enough!" He didn't like them

being spread out as they were, for that kind of formation boded no good.

One of the men had been slightly ahead of the others, the typical move of a leader, and he lifted his hand. "Whoa there, friend. We mean no harm!"

"Then how 'bout you close ranks, no reason for you to be spread out like that. Makes me a little uncomfortable."

The leader chuckled, glancing left to right at his men. He looked back at Reuben, grinning. "We're just headin' back to our cabin. Been to town to get supplies. We been doin' a little gold pannin' on the creek up yonder," nodding with his head to the upper end of the long valley that carried the Lodgepole creek. But Reuben saw no supplies nor evidence of gold- panning and they did not have the look of gold miners.

The man on the far right, a grizzled looking sort with shaggy beard, what there was of it, a floppy hat, dirty shirt, and corded britches, cackled as he spoke, "Hey, Smitty, that there redhead at the back, ain't she the kind you like with all that red hair and such?"

The others chortled and the one called Smitty snarled, "Shut up, Bull!"

The dirty one sat back in his saddle, both hands resting on the pommel and grumbled as he gave a sidelong glance to the leader. The man to the left of Smitty laughed. "I'll take that blonde there, she's just what I like!" He was a lean built man with a hat that was pinned up on one side with a feather and had eyes that were black beneath his thick eyebrows as they glinted with lust and evil.

"How 'bout you fellas move right along and quit your talkin' 'bout these ladies?!" growled Reuben.

"Well now, that don't seem fair," began the man that

sided Smitty. His bushy sideburns showed a touch of grey, and he wore a tattered Confederate cap. His flinty eyes glared over his grinning lips that accented his red bulb of a nose. His pot belly almost obscured the saddle horn and the matted mane of his horse told much about the man and his lack of concern for anyone or anything. "After all, there's only one o' you, and three women. While the four of us ain't got none!" his whiney voice made his words sound like a plea instead of a statement.

"And that's the way it's gonna stay, now move along!" demanded Reuben.

The leader was slowly moving his hand toward the pistol that sat behind his belt, until Reuben lifted his and said, "You touch that, it'll be the last thing you do!"

The man, suddenly sober, stayed his movement as he glared at Reuben. Then asked, "You really think you can take all four of us?"

"He won't have to!" came the threat from Elly as she brought the Henry to her shoulder, sighting on the one called Bull. "And before you try anything, Bull, know this. Before you could bring that shooter from your belt, you'll be lying on your back in a puddle of blood with your guts running into the creek yonder."

"And if you try anything, old man," snarled Sadie as she drew back the tomahawk shoulder high, "I can part your hair down to your nose with this!"

"Guess that leaves it up to you, Jonesy. Ain't no one focused on you!" whined the leader.

"He can try, but after I give you a third eye, I'll put a bullet into that tobacco tag hangin' from his pocket!" responded Reuben.

"And when he hits the ground, I'll claw his eyes out and spit in the sockets!" screamed Mabel, startling the others.

"Now, you ready to start this dance or you wanna go to your cabin?" asked Reuben.

"Easy now, easy," began the leader as he held his hands to the side. "We were just funnin', didn't mean no harm. We'll just move along now and let you go your way." He slowly reached for the reins that lay on the neck of his horse, spoke to his men, "Let's just go, men. These ladies don't seem to be interested in our comp'ny."

Reuben's breath was coming shallow, he knew the slightest move could set things off and he didn't want the ladies hurt, but he stared at the leader, watching his cautious moves. He knew these were bad men, fighters, probably used to taking what they wanted and let the devil take the high road, but things changed when Bull growled, "I ain't lettin' no woman..." as he reached for his pistol.

The Henry roared and the big man's solar plexus split like a dry twig, blood spouted a red blossom on his chest and the big man's chin dropped to his chest then lifted to Elly, "You kilt me!" and he slid to the ground.

Elly jacked another shell and swung the muzzle to the old man, but he was grabbing at the handle of the tomahawk that hung between his eyes. The blade was buried in his skull and his movement was reflexive as he fell onto the neck of his skittish mount. The horse side-stepped and bumped the riderless horse of the leader, and both horses crow hopped away from the pandemonium.

Reuben's pistol exploded with smoke and lead as he dropped the hammer on the leader. The man was grabbing for his pistol and the bullet took him high on the chest. He snagged the pistol from his belt and was lifting it as the second round from Reuben took him in the throat. His head snapped back, and he crumpled to the ground just as the old man's horse pushed his aside.

The last man had brought his pistol from his belt and snatched off a shot at Reuben, missing but close enough for Reuben to feel the heat of the passing bullet, yet before he could fire again, the Henry barked and carried death on a .44 caliber bullet to the hatchet-faced man. Red blossomed on his chest, and he stared down at the pulsing blood. He lifted his eyes to the blonde, a smile painting his face until the light faded from his eyes and he dropped his head to his chest, staying in his saddle as the skittish horse danced to the side and stood still.

The sudden quiet pierced the low-lying grey cloud of powder smoke as each of the four stared at the death that had been dealt by their hands. Stillness lay upon them like a dark blanket, wide eyes stared at the dead bodies that lay twisted on the ground as horses trotted away, trailing reins behind them. Sadie was the first to speak, "That's not how I thought this day would go." The others turned to look at her stunned by her response, but Reuben slowly shook his head, "It could have been a lot worse," he added, his voice barely above a whisper. He looked around, slipping the spare loaded cylinder for the Remington from his belt and replacing the partially used one with the fully loaded cylinder. He snapped the loading lever back and slid the revolver into his holster. "We'll need to bury 'em." He looked around and chose a dry gulch between two low rolling sand hills. "There. We'll drag 'em over, cave in the bank over the bodies, roll some rocks down on 'em." He was speaking to himself more than the others, expecting little help from the women, but he turned to them. "Sadie, you and Mabel try to catch up the horses, strip 'em of anythin' useful, and trail 'em back if they will." He turned to look at his wife. "How 'bout you takin' the mule to the trees yonder, and I'll be along shortly."

The women slowly moved to comply with Reuben's directions as he stepped down and wrapped the loop of his riata around the feet of the closest two men. He bent down and went through their pockets, finding little of use or purpose save a few greenbacks and coins, the leader had a pocket full of .36 caliber paper cartridges for his smaller framed Remington revolver. He swung back aboard, dallied the riata around the saddle horn and started for the dry gulch. He repeated his moves with the last two men, and once all were piled at the bottom of the wide gulch, he readily caved the ledge off to cover the bodies. He lifted several large stones from roundabout and rolled them onto the makeshift graves. Satisfied, he looked to the sky. "God, they're yours now, don't reckon you really want 'em, seein' as how they're closer to the devil as it is, but you're in charge, so..." He looked down at the caved in bank, mounted up and returned to the others.

He was surprised when he rode near where the women had tethered the horses and sat on a log looking at a pile of booty taken from the horses. They left the saddles on the three mounts they caught, and all the animals were tethered in the shade of a cluster of cottonwoods, but in a pile at their feet were several bags, saddle bags, and weapons. Reuben stepped down, looked at the women, then at the pile and asked, "What's all that?"

Sadie responded, "Looks like those fellas robbed the Overland stage. Those bags are full of gold and coins. Must be more'n three, four thousand dollars there, and all the bags are marked 'Clark, Gruber & Co. Bank and Mint.'"

Reuben pushed his hat to the back of his head,

scratching his forehead. "Whoooeee! Them fellas were meaner'n I thought."

"Ummhmm," added Elly, "but looks like you got another Sharps and I got me a pistol!" holding up a Colt Pocket revolver in .36 caliber.

"And we have rifles too!" declared Mabel, holding up a Henry and nodding to Sadie as she held up a Spencer.

"Looks like we'll need to return the gold to the stage line, but I reckon the weapons are yours. So, let's load up and get you home," nodding to the two women proudly holding their new rifles. Within moments, the band of four riders moved out, each one trailing an animal on lead with Reuben leading off with the mule following Blue and each of the women trailing one of the outlaws' horses. But their thoughts were not on the animals, but on the skirmish that had brought death to so many yet allowed them to escape what could have been an even worse fate.

A thin tendril of smoke rose from the black pile of rubble that had once stood as a landmark barn. Even the drivers of passing stages on the far side of the river would look for the barn that marked the halfway point between the stage stations. A stench of burned flesh lay upon the rubble while the few horses crowded the far rails of the corral fence. It was quiet when the four riders approached, although it was mid-afternoon and the sun was high in the clear blue sky, an afternoon that would usually herald the activity of the ranch's cowboys. Some would be working with the yearling horses, others coming in from the far pastures after tending the cattle, and one or more would be in the shady barn mending gear.

The porch of the ranch house would usually have at least one woman in a rocking chair or sitting at a loom or spinning wheel. But the porch was void of life and the rocking chair sat still. The four reined up until Sadie pushed forward, forehead wrinkled with a frown as she shaded her eyes to search for any survivors of the attack..

The bunkhouse door stood ajar, and the foreman's house showed no sign of life.

The door of the ranch house creaked open a few inches and a rifle barrel protruded. "Who are you and whaddaya want?" came the voice of a woman, fear adding a crackly tenor to the words.

"Ma? Ma? Is that you, Ma?" cried Sadie, gigging her horse forward.

The door pushed open a little farther, an ashen pale face showed, and the voice asked, "Sadie? Oh, bless Jesus, it is you! Sadie, my girl! We thought you was taken by the Injuns!" The woman pushed her way past the half-open door, put the rifle across the arms of the rocking chair and turned with arms stretched wide as she watched her daughter slip from the horse and come running to the porch. She took the steps two at a time and was enveloped in the arms of her mother, both shedding tears like an April rain on a tin roof.

Reuben chuckled as he sat beside Elly who had teared up with a broad smile and watched the reunion. Mabel had ridden her mount close to the porch and asked, "Are my folks to home?"

Sadie's mother pushed away from her daughter. "Your Ma's there, but your Pa and brother went with the hired hands to try to find you!" Mabel reined the mount around and slapped legs to the horse's ribs to take off to the foreman's house at a run, anxious to see her mother.

Sadie frowned as she looked at her mother, afraid to speak her thoughts but asked, "And Pa? Did he go too?"

Her mother turned toward her and slowly shook her head. "No, dear, your Pa was kilt by the Injuns." The women fell into one another's arms, sobbing and shaking and they clung to one another, until a younger girl, about twelve, came from the house and tugged on the women's arms, wanting to be included in the circle of sadness.

Sadie pulled away, wiping her face, and turned toward Reuben and Elly, then back to her mother. "Ma, I want you to meet some friends. This is Reuben and Elly, they saved us from the Cheyenne."

Reuben touched the brim of his hat, nodding, and said, "Ma'am, pleased to meet you."

Elly nodded and added, "Yes, Ma'am, we are pleased to meet you."

The woman turned toward them, wiping her hands on her apron, and using the hem to wipe her eyes. "Pardon my manners, please, get down and come in the house."

"Pleased to, Ma'am, but I need to take care of these horses first, but my wife'll join you," answered Reuben, swinging down from Blue and gathering up the lead lines of the other horses and his mule. He led the bunch to the corral and opened the pole gate, led them in and dropped the lines to shut the gate. His practiced hands wasted little time stripping the gear and hanging it on the top rail of the fence, checked the water and worked the pump to add some fresh, saw some hay stacked at the far end and fetched a pitchfork and forked some hay to all the horses. He gave them all a quick rubdown with a handful of the grass hay, spending a little extra time with Blue, and Elly's Appy, and satisfied, left the corral for the ranch house.

As he walked into the house, the women were sitting on a settee and chairs and looked up as he entered. Sadie's mother, Ethel, jumped to her feet and quickly walked to Reuben, drew him into a hug and said, "Thank you, thank you, thank you. I could never do enough to thank you for saving my daughter and Mabel!"

Reuben was a little surprised and leaned back to look at the woman. "It wasn't just me, ma'am, my wife was in the bushes with her rifle on those Cheyenne."

She spun on her heel and reached for Elly, giving her a big hug as well. She leaned back, still holding on to Elly and forced a smile. "Now, I'm going to fix you a big supper!" but both girls joined in and within moments, Reuben had been ushered to the porch and the rocking chair with a cup of coffee, and the preparations and conversation hummed in the kitchen.

A lop-eared mutt padded carefully up the steps, head hanging and eyes downcast, and came beside the chair and flopped on his belly, cradling his chin between his paws. Reuben dropped a hand to stroke the dog's neck and ears and said, "Well, hello pooch! Hope you don't mind if I use your master's rockin' chair," and with those words he realized the loss the family had suffered. But he knew Sadie was a strong woman and if her mother were cut from the same cloth, they would be just fine. The ranch was well-kept, of course the barn would have to be rebuilt, but with a foreman and his son, plus two hired hands, they should get the job done.

He sipped his coffee as he thought about the past few days, thinking this was the first time he had slowed down enough to relax and feel a little safe. He also thought about the money they took from the outlaws and thought about where they could turn it in, and if there was a lawman anywhere near, they should report the killing of the men. But that could wait until after they had a good meal and maybe a good night's sleep.

REUBEN PUSHED BACK FROM THE TABLE, PATTED HIS BELLY and said, "Ma'am, that was a mighty fine meal! It's been some time since I've had beefsteak, and that was delicious, however, I do believe that crab apple pie topped everythin'!"

"Why, thank you Reuben. I always enjoy cooking for someone that appreciates a fine meal."

Elly smiled at Reuben as she reached for her coffee cup. Everyone had crowded around the table, including Mabel and her mother, Gladys. Mabel smiled as she looked at Reuben and Elly. "And my mother's specialty is flapjacks, and she's expecting all of you to her house for breakfast!"

"That sounds fine!" answered Reuben, "but we need to get an early start to make Julesburg. I'd like to meet with the superintendent of the stage line and see about maybe gettin' a job with the line." No one had mentioned the set-to they had with the outlaws, and they saw no reason to add the weight of concern to the already fretful mothers. Reuben and the others had talked about the best place to turn in the bags of gold would be the main office in Julesburg, and there would probably be a marshal there that should be told about the outlaws.

"Well, we," started Sadie, nodding to Mabel, "should probably go with you so we can replace those rags we left at the river. After using Elly's clothes, we probably ought to get her a replacement or two as well."

Elly laughed. "I don't think I'll need those dresses where we're going and doing what we'll be doing, whatever that may be, but these," she plucked at the buckskin tunic she wore, "seem to suit me just fine!"

Sadie leaned over and touched Elly's arm. "But I heard about these new outfits that have split skirts to make it easy for riding; maybe that would be useful to you!"

Elly frowned, "Split skirts?"

"Ummhmm, and the dressmaker in Julesburg was making one for me and I'm sure she could make one for you too!" she added conspiratorially as she winked.

Elly laughed, and spoke softly, "And you wondered why he called you a she-bear!" The three girls giggled together, betraying their mischievous and girlish side. Sadie's mother had listened in and smiling, said, "That sounds like something your father would say," and the laughing stopped.

Sadie asked her mother, "When did everyone leave to try to find us?"

"Right after the attack was over. They helped bury your Pa and left soon after. They followed their trail through the upper pasture, and near as I could tell, they took the draw with Cottonwood Creek, but after that, I don't know. I reckon they planned to follow their trail."

Sadie looked at Reuben. "You think they could tell what happened by the sign?"

"Depends on if there's a decent tracker among 'em."

Sadie looked at Mabel and her mother. "Your man's a good tracker, and so's Bert, aren't they?"

Gladys nodded, glancing at Mabel, who added, "Bert is the better of the two, and I think he could track a mosquito across a pond!"

Sadie looked back at Reuben, who answered, "I think they could make out what happened. They could tell where the trail split, and we came south while the Cheyenne kept to the north. But, that last run in we had this mornin' with them fellas, well, that might confuse 'em a mite, but they could prob'ly figger things out. If they were close behind the Cheyenne, and not too far back on our trail, they might show up just any time. If not, well, I might have to go lookin'."

37

Sadie looked back at her mother. "Maybe we oughta be praying for 'em, ya reckon?"

Her mother patted her hand. "I been praying ever since you didn't come home, and He brought you back, so I reckon He'll bring them back as well!" Sadie smiled and looked from Reuben to Elly and to the other women, nodding her head to each one as if that settled things.

The bunkhouse was a small cabin, two sets of bunks and a pot-bellied stove just big enough to heat a pot of coffee and keep the chill off the one room. Reuben was stoking a fire in the stove when he turned and asked, "You want a top bunk or bottom?" grinning at Elly. She smiled and tossed her bedroll on the bottom bunk and looked coyly at her husband, who stood up from the stove and looked at her as she answered, "We'll take the bottom bunk!" putting her hand through the crook of his arm.

"Well, alright then!" he responded, smiling down at his little blonde.

The door creaked open, and two men stomped into the darkness of the bunkhouse. One said, "Hey, there's a fire in the stove!"

"I reckon Ma Slade started it, hopin' we'd be back sooner'n later," replied the second man as he started to sit on the first bunk. He jumped when he saw someone sitting up under the covers. "Hey! Who're you?" growled the man, stepping close to the stove and opening the stove door to let the light from the fire illuminate the room. He looked at his partner. "Get a candle!" he ordered. He looked back at the man in the bunk, who was rubbing his eyes with one hand as he lay the pistol on his lap with the other.

"Name's Reuben. Reuben Grundy. Who're you?"

"We work here, and it's my bunk you're in!"

"What's all the noise?" asked Elly from behind Reuben.

"What'chu got back there? That a woman?" asked the second man, leaning toward the bunk with the candle that still was not lit.

"She's my wife!" declared Reuben.

39

"Ain't s'posed to be no wimmen in here!" complained the first man.

"We couldn't sleep in the barn, now could we?" asked Elly, peeking over Reuben's shoulder.

"Well, I reckon that's one way to warm your bunk," replied the second man. He looked at his partner, back at Reuben, "By the way, I'm Jeremiah Cash, and this is my brother, Dustan." He reached down to shake Reuben's hand, "And if you're Reuben, who's the blonde?"

Reuben shook their hands, and chuckling said, "She's Elly, my wife."

"You said that already. So, I reckon those horses in the corral are yours?"

"Some, couple of 'em are the girls'."

Jeremiah frowned. "The girls?"

"Sadie and Mabel."

"You brought 'em home?" he asked, incredulous as he sat back on the stool beside the stove.

"Both of 'em?" asked Dustan.

"Yup," answered Reuben, squirming around to face the brothers.

"How'd you get 'em from the Injuns?" asked Jeremiah.

"Traded my rifle for 'em."

"Traded? You traded a rifle for 'em?"

"Too many of 'em to shoot, so I thought I'd try tradin'. The leader, Tall Bull, fancied my rifle so we struck a deal for the girls and their horses, course I had to throw in a tomahawk and a knife, but it was easier than fightin' all of 'em."

He heard Elly snicker behind him as she playfully slapped his back. "Yeah, but I was hiding in the bushes, and I had the only rifle and only fourteen cartridges and there were twelve Indians and I mighta missed one!" she explained.

The two brothers looked at one another, shaking their heads, and Jeremiah said, "Would you mind turnin' to the window so we can get our duds off and get in bed. I think this tale would be better listened to in the daylight!"

Elly giggled and bounced around to face the wall and said, "I'm facing the wall, but hurry up, I wanna get some sleep, and you're so noisy!"

The boys groaned as they struggled to pull off their boots and drop their britches and such. They bounded into their bunks and Dustan said, "Alright, we're in bed, but what about in the mornin' when we need to go to the outhouse?"

"Keep your eyes closed," answered Elly, giggling.

ALTHOUGH THE RIVERBED WAS WIDE AND SANDY, THE channel of the river was a little over a hundred fifty feet wide, but at no place was the water any more than a couple feet deep. The river often divided, making two wandering streams that kept to the wide bed, making for fertile though sandy and gravelly soil. The crossing below the ranch was across a gravelly bottom with the slow current barely knee deep on the horses. It was the same four that were bound for Julesburg, Reuben, Elly, and the girls from the ranch, Sadie, and Mabel. But the mood today was much different than the days before, they were full of gaiety and talked all the while.

It soon became evident that the girls had set their caps for the ranch hand brothers, and Sadie had put her dibs on Jeremiah. The older brother was only three years her senior while Dustan only had a year on Mabel. "Dustan said there was going to be a dance in town this Saturday, are you going to get a new dress?" asked

Mabel, glancing at her friend as they came from the water and their horses did the belly roll to rid themselves of what little water had splashed on their bellies.

"Maybe; Jeremiah has seen most of my other dresses, but I'm anxious to get that split skirt mostly," replied Sadie, laughing as she nudged her mount through the blossoming chokecherry bushes. The girls continued with their chatter as they rode, and Elly heard enough to be reminded of the times she went to dances and such back in Iowa before her family sold the farm. She glanced over to Reuben, smiled happily, knowing that her life had changed, but it was for the better and she was glad to have the silliness of girlhood behind her and the promise of the future with her husband before them.

"What if you can't get on with the stage line, then what?" she asked Reuben, glancing from him to the road traveled by the wagon trains and the stages.

"Oh, I dunno. Nothin' to worry about though, I've got a little money saved up and stashed away. And like the pastor said, if we trust in the Lord, the Lord will provide."

"So, does that mean you two will go to church with us tomorrow?" asked Sadie, leaning forward as she spoke.

"Church? Tomorrow? Is today Saturday?" asked Reuben.

"It is! And yes, there is church tomorrow, and our families will come in for the day. So, it would be nice if you two would join us."

"Well, we'll just see what we can do about that," agreed Reuben, winking at Elly who smiled back at her man. They had never been in church together and she was pleased with his answer. It would be nice to join with others in a regular service, for she had always enjoyed their times in worship. That was why she and her mother had been so surprised that her father had joined with the Mormons to make the trek west, but that was behind her now and she looked forward to a time together with her new friends.

Reuben and Elly were surprised at the size of the town of Julesburg. "I didn't expect much more than a tradin' post and stage station, but that first buildin' there is the original tradin' post that Sadie said was built by that fella, Jules Beni, who had later become an outlaw and was killed by Sadie's Uncle Jack." He chuckled as he remembered her tale of the capture of Beni by her uncle. He pointed out the two-story hotel with a saloon on the ground floor. "We'll get us a room there, since we're stayin' for church."

Elly smiled and let her eyes take in the town. On their right she pointed out, "That must be the dressmaker there," and turned to Sadie. "Is that the store with the dressmaker?"

"Ummhmm, her name is Bessie and she's very good. Her husband owns the store," answered Sadie. There was a restaurant beside the store and Reuben suggested, "If you ladies want to go to the dressmaker, I'll go to the stage station and meet with the station keeper. We can meet up at the restaurant in about an hour if that suits?"

Elly twisted around in her saddle to look at the girls who were smiling and nodding. She looked to Reuben. "That sounds fine."

"Oh," and he reached into his pocket and withdrew a couple coins to hand to Elly, "you get whatever you want."

She accepted the coins, and her eyes flared as she looked back up at Reuben. She whispered, "These are twenty-dollar gold pieces!"

"Uh, yeah. Is that not enough?"

"I could buy the store for this!"

Reuben smiled. "I don't think so, but maybe you can help Mabel; I don't think she has too much."

Elly smiled, glancing back at her friends and reined her Appy to the hitchrail. As the girls stepped down, Reuben continued to the stage station that stood at the far end of town, between the livery and a warehouse. He stopped in front of the station but saw the hitchrail at the side and moved Blue to the side to tether him and the mule. He walked into the station where a long counter separated the front of the station with benches for passengers, from the desks for the clerks. He stepped to the counter, rapped on the plank top to get the attention of two men that were visiting, one sitting on the corner of a desk and the other seated behind the desk. The seated man looked up, "Yes?" he asked, appearing annoyed.

"Who's in charge?" asked Reuben.

"Why do you ask?" replied the seated agent.

"I want to talk to the station keeper or superintendent," answered Reuben, forcing himself to remain civil when his first inclination was to move around the counter and jerk the impudent clerk up by his collar and slap some sense and courtesy into him.

The taller man that had sat on the corner of the desk stood and came to the counter. "I'm William Buckley, I'm the superintendent for this stretch. What can I help you with?"

"Have you had some robberies of your stages recently?" asked Reuben.

The man frowned, and slowly nodded his head, his eyes narrowing as he looked at the man before him, suspicious of his intent and questions. "Yes, we have," he answered slowly.

"Then I've got something for you. If you gentlemen would give me a hand," explained Reuben as he turned away, motioning for the two men to follow.

The one called Buckley motioned to the seated man and they followed Reuben from the building. When Reuben unstrapped the panniers and reached in to pull out the first of the four bags and hand it to the super, the man's eyes flared and he smiled broadly, "Where'd you get this?"

Reuben did not answer but reached for the other bags, handing one to the second man and taking the other two himself. He nodded to the station and the two men moved quickly into the building. Buckley called out, "Mr. Holladay! Mr. Holladay!"

The door to the back room opened and a distinguished looking man with a stern expression came through, frowning and bellowed, "What? What are you hollering about?"

Buckley plopped the first bag on the counter, followed by the one from the clerk and the two from Reuben. Buckley said, "This is the gold from the last robbery! I believe it's all there!"

Holladay's expression changed as he stepped close and quickly opened the first bag to look at the gold and coin. He looked up at Buckley who nodded toward Reuben. "This man just brought it in."

Holladay looked at Reuben. "Young man, you are an answer to prayer! Thank you! Where did you get this?" nodding toward the bags on the counter.

"Well, we ran into some disagreeable sorts and after we had a long talk, they kinda left it behind."

B en Holladay had motioned Reuben to join him in the back office and Reuben was surprised to see another man, already seated, and waiting. Holladay walked behind the desk and took his seat as he motioned Reuben to the empty chair beside the other man. "Reuben Grundy, this is Theodore W. Moses, a friend of mine from Missouri." He looked at Moses, "Ted, this is Reuben Grundy. Mr. Grundy just brought in the entire gold shipment that was so recently stolen in the hold-up between Beaver Creek and Valley Station."

Moses frowned, looked at Reuben and back to Holladay, "You don't say! This youngster?" He shook his head and turned to Reuben, "So, how many men were there with you?"

"None, but my wife and two young ladies that had an extended visit with the Cheyenne Dog Soldiers under Tall Bull, were with me and did their part."

"Well, how many highwaymen were in the gang that did the robbery?"

"That I couldn't say, I wasn't there. But there were four that we met on the trail, the four that had the gold

46

shipment." Reuben was getting a little antsy and twisted in his seat to look at Holladay. "If that's all you need, Mr. Holladay, I'll be goin'," and started to get up from the chair, but Holladay motioned him to stay seated as he grinned at Moses.

Moses shook his head looking from Reuben to Holladay, "I dunno if I can believe this or not," and looked at Reuben with one eyebrow cocked up as he squinted his eyes looking sideways at him. "So, you and three women convinced these men to just hand over the gold?"

"Well, no. We didn't know they had it, until we started to bury 'em, and the girls discovered it on the horses." Reuben was enjoying the banter with the men, knowing they were having a hard time understanding or believing what he was saying, but truth be known, whenever he gave it much thought, it was a little hard for him to believe.

Moses became frustrated and jumped to his feet and strode to the window to look out, his back to the others as he mumbled to himself. He turned around, "So, they were already dead when you came upon them, musta been, because by all reports these were dangerous desperados, and I just don't see how you and three women..."

Reuben grinned. "No, they were rude and ill-mannered and both me and the women asked them politely to mind their manners, but when they didn't, well, when the smoke cleared three were dead from gunshots and one had a hatchet buried in his skull, and of course he was dead too."

"Are you telling me you shot four men who were trying to kill you?" stammered the frustrated Moses.

"No, no. I only shot one. My wife, Elly, shot two, and

Sadie, one of the girls that were captives of the Cheyenne, threw the hatchet at the other'n."

Moses looked at Holladay and both men looked wide-eyed at Reuben. Holladay said, "It was easier to believe *you* shot 'em all!"

"And you buried them all?" asked Moses, returning to his seat.

"Yessir."

"Well, I'd have to see the bodies 'fore we could pay any reward!" he declared, looking at Holladay.

"Of course, of course," replied Holladay. He turned to Reuben, "Could you take Marshal Moses to see the graves, Reuben?"

The title of marshal made things a bit more clear for Reuben, considering the questioning the man had subjected him to and Reuben nodded. "I could tell you where they are just as easy, if you'd like, but I can't be leavin' my wife."

"Based on what you just told us, it doesn't sound like she'd be in any danger," replied the Marshal. "You understand, I can't authorize any bounty to be paid unless I see the bodies?"

"Bounty? I wasn't expectin' any bounty."

Holladay grinned, nodding. "Mr. Grundy, you will get a reward for returning the gold of ten percent, that will be close to five hundred dollars. And the reward on the four outlaws was two hundred fifty dollars on each one."

A low whistle came from Reuben as he sat forward on the chair, looking from Holladay to Moses. "Well, I reckon I can take you to the graves for that kind of money. And I was just comin' in here to ask for a job!"

Holladay and Moses looked to one another, and Reuben noticed a slight nod that passed between them before the owner of the Overland Stage Line looked at

Reuben. "That's exactly what we were considering for you, Reuben."

Moses scooted his chair around to face Reuben. "But first, I need to ask you a few things, is that alright?"

"Sure, sure," replied Reuben.

"First, how did you happen to be here at this time, you know, to run into the outlaws when you did?" asked the marshal.

Reuben began, "Well, when I mustered out of Berdan's Sharpshooters, I headed home to my folk's place in White Pigeon, Michigan." He breathed a heavy sigh and continued, detailing the deaths of his family, his pursuit of the Home Guard renegades, his run-in with the Bushwhackers as he guided the wagons to Fort Kearny, and the more recent set-to with gunrunners and the different native tribes. He finished with, "And here I am."

"Young man, you've lived more in your short life than most men see in twice the years that you have had," declared Ben Holladay, looking from Reuben to the marshal.

The two men nodded to one another, and the marshal looked at Reuben. "Here's what we need, Reuben. You see, ever since the Overland Stage line has been hauling gold for the banks and gold fields of Colorado, there has been an increasing number of hold-ups and we think it has to do with the war. There is a certain element of Confederate sympathizers that have organized down around Pueblo and Cañon City, and we think they are behind the robberies. Their purpose, of course, is to provide gold for the South, but the Union needs that same gold. Now what we are thinking..." and he outlined the plan of using Reuben as a deputy marshal, but without anyone knowing. His authority would only extend to the stage line and its operations with the sole purpose of preventing the theft of gold and money shipments, or the recovery of any stolen goods.

"You would ride the stages as you see fit, or work through the stations or be completely independent, if you prefer. But we think you are the man for the job. You haven't been here long enough for anyone to know you, and you could travel incognito at any time. You will have complete authority. You see, I'm the marshal for Missouri, and I'm here only because Mr. Holladay is a friend and he asked for my help."

"But why isn't there a marshal for Colorado territory?" asked Reuben, frowning.

Holladay chuckled. "There was, for a while. A fella by the name of Copeland Townsend served a while, then Governor Gilpin replaced him with Cameron Hunt, then he was removed, and he was going to appoint another marshal, but he was relieved of his position, and now Governor Evans is more concerned with raising a militia for the war than he is about the problem we have. But he knows the marshal here and has agreed to abide by whatever he thinks is best."

"Well, I was lookin' for a job, but, well, I've got a couple questions," he paused as he looked at the men, "First, I want my wife with me at all times, so does she need to be deputized also?"

The marshal grinned. "If she can shoot as good as you say, that won't be a problem."

Reuben nodded. "And do I need papers or a badge of somethin' showin' I have the authority to arrest the outlaws?"

Moses grinned as he reached into the outside pocket of his jacket and brought out a silver badge, a circle with a five-pointed star in the center and the words *Deputy*

United States Marshal imprinted around the rim. He handed it to Reuben and stood, motioning Reuben to stand as well. The men faced one another, and the marshal said, "Raise your right hand and repeat after me." Reuben nodded and raised his hand as the marshal began, "I, Reuben Grundy," and paused after each phrase for Reuben to repeat, "do solemnly swear that I will faithfully execute all lawful precepts, directed to the Marshal of the United States for the Territory of Colorado, under the authority..." and continued through the oath, then concluded with, "so help me God."

The men shook hands all around, and the marshal said, "I'll have a printed copy of that for you tomorrow and you'll need to sign it for our records."

"And my wife?" asked Reuben.

"And your wife," grinned the marshal. "And when do we get to meet this sharpshooter you call your wife?"

"Well, I've got to meet her and the girls at the restaurant when I leave here, so, you gentlemen are welcome to join us," offered Reuben.

"Good, good," declared the marshal, "and that will give us time to make plans to go to the graves of the outlaws, and perhaps make some plans for coming days." He looked from Reuben to Holladay and received a nod of agreement. "So, we will join you shortly."

Reuben shook hands with both men again, thanking them for the rewards and the opportunity, and turned away, shaking his head at the strange turn of events, but pleased with the promise of the future. He smiled as he thought of his wife as a deputy marshal and shook his head as he left the stage station, wondering how she was going to take the news of their new mission.

"That's the reward for returning the shipment!" declared the man as he stood beside the table with Reuben and the girls. He smiled broadly. "I'm Ben Holladay of the Overland Stage Line and we greatly appreciate what you have done for us!"

Reuben smiled as he watched the reaction of the girls, standing from his chair beside Elly. "Ladies, as he said, this is Mr. Holladay, and this other gentleman is Theodore Moses, Federal Marshal out of Missouri." He motioned to his wife, "Gentlemen, this is my wife Elly, and these ladies are Sadie Slade and Mabel Masengale."

Both men doffed their hats and nodded to the ladies, Holladay the first to speak, "Pleased to meet you, ladies!" and was echoed by the marshal, "Yes, pleased indeed!"

"Won't you join us, gentlemen?" asked Elly, motioning to the chairs at the end of the table.

The newcomers gladly accepted the offer and were seating themselves as all three women turned to Reuben as Elly asked, "Reward?" as she hefted the leather pouch heavy with gold coin.

"I was gonna tell you, I just didn't have a chance. You

were all so excited about the dresses and dance I couldn't get a word in edgewise! We can split it up later," he said as he nodded toward the men.

"So, does this mean I'll have enough money to get that dress?" whispered Mabel, looking at Reuben.

He grinned. "And then some," he answered.

"So, are you ladies going to the dance tomorrow evening?" asked Holladay, leaning his elbows on the table to look at the bouquet of pretty ladies.

"Yes, Mr. Holladay, our beaus, the brothers Cash, are coming in from the ranch and we'll go together," said Sadie, smiling as the waitress brought the first of their meals. "And could you explain about this reward? Reuben failed to mention it."

Holladay chuckled. "Of course. It's just our company's way of showing our appreciation for the return of stolen goods. It's the usual reward of ten percent and in this case, that amounted to almost five hundred dollars!"

The three girls gasped, Sadie having to use her napkin to keep from spitting out the sip of coffee she had taken, as they looked wide-eyed at the man. "Five hundred dollars?" she asked, incredulous.

"That's correct, and it's all in gold coin."

"And there's more," added Reuben. "There was a reward on those outlaws. We," motioning to the marshal and himself, "will ride out tomorrow so he can see who they were, then if he agrees, there will be a bit more coming our way."

All the women were smiling and chattering among themselves, and all the men heard were snippets of conversation, mostly about dresses and the dance. The men looked at one another, the marshal shaking his head as he looked to Holladay, "Oh, to be young again!"

The men chuckled and Moses looked at Reuben. "What time do you want to leave in the morning?"

"Break of day would be best. It'll take us about three hours to get there and my wife wants me back for the dance," he answered, nodding toward Elly, and smiling.

She turned to him and said, "You better be back in time. This is our first dance, don't forget!"

"Yes, ma'am," he answered, reaching for his coffee.

"THE LAST TIME I WAS AT A DANCE LIKE THIS, I RECKON I was about twelve. I do remember gettin' in a bit of a fight over a little redhead girl, and for the life of me, I can't even remember her name!" chuckled Reuben as he escorted Elly up the steps of the town hall. Folks had come from miles around, buggies and buckboards were parked nearby, and the hitch rails held more horses than intended. The ladies were in their best dresses, and men were cleaned up and dressed up, and most had shaved, and some had shined their boots.

As they stepped into the hall, the band was tuning up and getting acquainted and Reuben was surprised at the number of instruments and musicians. He saw a big bull fiddle with a skinny man that probably stood about six and half feet strumming on the strings. A colored man held a banjo, and another darkie had a fiddle and the two were talking and laughing. Elly saw him looking at the band and said, "The girls told me there was a very musical family from Italy; that looks like them on the left there." The ones she indicated had a guitar, a lute, a mandolin, and a fiddle. Behind them sat a man, arms crossed and holding some drumsticks, behind a set of drums and watching the others.

"There's more in that band than I've ever seen

before," observed Reuben as they walked to the benches that lined the walls. "Here's hopin' they sound good!"

"Even if they don't, it'll still be fun," retorted Elly, laughing as they joined Sadie and Mabel who sat with the Cash brothers.

"Howdy Reuben!" greeted Jeremiah. "You set for this dancin'?"

"Dunno, ain't been to one since I was about twelve," replied Reuben, red rising on his neck as he was already embarrassed just thinking about dancing.

Elly bumped against him. "Oh, you'll be fine. 'Sides, it don't make any difference. Prob'ly ain't nobody here can dance any better. We're all here for fun!" She leaned forward to look past Reuben to Sadie. "Ain't that right, Sadie?"

"That's right, Elly!" she answered as she stood and pulled Jeremiah to his feet. The band was starting with *When Johnny Comes Marching Home*, and she wanted to get the first dance. The others quickly joined her, and the fun began.

The band started off lively and the people responded with dancing, swinging, and singing. After *Wait for the Wagon*, they slowed the tempo with *Lorena and Kathleen Mavourneen*, but picked things back up with *The Girl I Left Behind Me*. A few more songs brought a break for the band and several folks stepped outside for some fresh air and a bit of moonlight. Suddenly a ruckus brought most from the hall into the street when a fight broke out. Reuben stepped to the edge of the crowd, Elly in tow, and saw Jeremiah Cash fighting toe to toe with the tall skinny man that had been playing the Bull Fiddle, but the contest was short-lived, and Jeremiah extended his hand to help the lanky figure from the ground, smiling and saying, "Ah, Bugs, ain't no reason to fight. She done said I'm the one she's gonna marry, so, let's be friends."

The tall man on the ground looked up, "Well, Jeremiah, we been friends a long time so ain't no sense lettin' a woman come 'tween us," and accepted the offered hand. The crowd quickly broke up and filed back into the hall to enjoy the rest of the night and finish the dance. Reuben and Elly walked behind Jeremiah and Dustan and heard Dustan ask, "Marry? She said she was gonna marry you?"

"Ummhmm, and that ain't all, she's already talkin' about a double weddin' to include you an' Mabel!"

"Now hold on there! I ain't said nuthin' 'bout gettin' married! I'm too young!" pleaded Dustan.

Elly chided the two, "You're older'n I am, Dustan, and I'm already married!"

He turned and looked at Elly. "But that's different!" he whined.

"Why?" asked Reuben.

"Well, cuz, that's all," he complained, kicking at a stone as he jammed his hands in his pockets.

The band brought things to a close with *Listen to the Mocking Bird* and a somber crowd drifted away, some to their rigs or horses, others to their homes. Reuben and Elly started to the hotel, followed close behind by Jeremiah, Sadie, Dustan and Mabel, each couple walking hand in hand and sharing intimate thoughts. As Reuben and Elly stepped through the doorway, the boys stood on the steps to say their good night, and Elly smiled as she heard Sadie remind the boys, "Don't forget, we're going to church in the morning!"

· · ·

THE PASTOR HAD PREACHED HIS SERMON FROM I Corinthians 6:20, *For ye are bought with a price: therefore glorify God in your body and in your spirit, which are God's.* "Now remember, friends, that is the purpose of our life, to glorify God! But as I've said, it is impossible glorify God if you don't know Jesus as your Savior. We must be born again to be a part of the family of God, and remember, to be born again, here's what you need to know. First, all of us are sinners! *Romans 3:10* and because we're sinners, there's a penalty for that sin, which is death and hell forever! *Romans 6:23* But, God doesn't want you to have to pay that penalty, that's why He sent His son, Jesus, to pay that penalty for you! *Romans 5:12* And when He paid that penalty, he also bought you and me a free gift, and that gift is eternal life! *Romans 6:23.* But, just like any other gift, it's a gift that must be received! *John 1:12* And to receive Him, we just call on Him in prayer, ask for forgiveness of our sins and to receive that gift of eternal life. *Romans 10:9-13*

"Now, if there's anyone here that has not received that gift and would like to, then as we begin to sing, just step out from your seat and come forward and let one of our men show you these scriptures and lead you in prayer that you might be born again and make certain of Heaven!"

The organist began playing and the people began to sing, *Just As I Am.* As they sang, there was a shuffling among the crowd, a few muffled whispers, and Sadie, holding Jeremiah's hand, led him down the aisle, followed by Dustan and Mabel. They were greeted by the pastor, and each couple was joined by one of the deacons of the church, and they knelt, talked, and prayed. As the song finished, the two couples stood together with two other men that had also come forward, and the pastor introduced them to the crowd. As he gave their names and said, "These young men have accepted Christ as their Savior this morning! If you're happy about their decision, say Amen!"

The crowd rocked the rafters with a loud "Amen!" and folks, including Reuben and Elly, crowded the front of the church to greet and encourage the men. The pastor had also announced that after the dinner on the grounds, they would go down to the river and baptize the men, which elicited another hearty "Amen!" from the crowd.

The crack of the black snake bullwhip sounded like a shot that echoed between the buildings. The mules lunged into their collars, the hames standing tall as the traces pulled taut and the coach rocked back on its thoroughbraces as the Jehu slapped the ribbons on the rumps of the mules, shouting encouragement to the fresh team. Reuben and Elly were pushed back against the thin cushion on the rear bench inside the coach. This was the first time for either of them to ride inside a stagecoach.

It started as an exciting escapade, but any sense of adventure was soon smothered with the powdery dust that filtered through the covered windows, the roll-up curtains doing little more than keeping the dust in rather than out. There were nine passengers crowded inside the coach, with two more 'hangers-on' up top. Reuben sat next to the window, Elly in the middle, and a matronly woman to her left. The middle row, whose backs were to them, held three men, one a cowboy of sorts and two that were attired like drummers. The three on the front row and facing to the back were an older couple, and a single man that was attired like a professional gambler with a satin waistcoat, a frocked coat that matched his striped britches, spat covered shoes, and a beaver felt top hat.

There was little conversation among the passengers, the dust and constant noise of creaking thoroughbraces, rattle of coach doors, rumble of wheels on the corduroy road, and the constant shouts and crack of the bullwhip from the Jehu up top, doing little to encourage the usual get-acquainted banter. It was uncomfortable with little room inside the coach, every available space taken up with bundles and bags of mail and packages stuffed under the seats, making the leg room non-existent. The short stops at the swing stations offered little more than quick trips to the outhouse or a short drink from the creaky pump at the well.

The second stop was at the Spring Hill station, a home station that offered meals, and when Reuben and Elly came from the coach, she looked back at the stage, then to Reuben. "How's about we trade places with those two that have been riding up top? I think the air up there would be a sight better!"

Reuben frowned as he looked at his bride, prompting her to explain, she chuckled, "Between that perfume on the woman next to me, and the smell of those two drummers that probably haven't had a bath since they started this journey back in St. Joseph, I can't hardly breathe! I'm used to fresh air and sunshine, not stink and dust!"

Reuben laughed, nodded. "You get us some food, I'll talk to the driver and shotgunner."

He walked to where the Jehu and shotgunner were helping the hostlers with the harness and gear for the new team, and Reuben asked the driver, "What do we need to do to trade places with those two ridin' up top?"

The driver turned to face Reuben, frowning, "You want to trade places?" he asked, "Ain't you travelin' with a woman?"

"That's right, she's my wife and asked if we could trade. She's not used to tight quarters and smelly bodies."

The Jehu laughed. "I can shore unnerstand that! I don't think there'd be a problem, seein' as how the inside seats are favored by most folks." He paused. "I'll arrange it."

The stop had lasted no more than twenty minutes, the meal was bacon, beans, and biscuits, and the team was raring to go as they pranced in place, mouthing the bits, and rattling the trace chains. Elly sat atop the coach, Reuben just behind the Jehu and shotgunner, his feet behind the men and as the coach rocked back, Elly was already making herself comfortable as she arranged the saddles and bags atop the coach. While they rode inside, most passengers kept their rifles and pistols handy in case of Indian attack, as did Reuben and Elly, but they had extra weapons bundled with scabbards and a blanket up top. They held on to their Henrys, Reuben had purchased a new one together with a Colt revolving shotgun and a Spencer repeater at Julesburg, but the other rifles and extra ammunition were bundled and lay with the gear atop the coach.

Elly bought a holster for her Colt pocket revolver and now wore it under her jacket on her left hip much like Reuben wore his Remington Army revolver. She had also added a custom-made Flemish knife and sheath that she wore between her shoulder blades with just the butt of the haft protruding above her collar but hidden by her hair. She paid a princely sum for the knife, but it was finely crafted and fit her hand perfectly. The balance of the knife made it perfect for throwing, and the blade was razor sharp. Reuben turned to see his woman curling up among the baggage and preparing for a nap, and he shook his head and smiled at his woman, who had changed almost daily since the day they met.

As the coach rocked on its way, Reuben saw the shotgunner point out the burned barn beside the ranch house across the river and tell the driver, "Musta been some renegades; that's recent!"

"Yeah, hadn't heard nuthin' 'bout it!" answered the driver.

Reuben joined in, "It was Cheyenne Dog Soldiers; they killed the rancher, captured the two girls, and took off. They lost five or six, but the girls were rescued and returned." He spoke loudly to overcome the rattle of trace chains and rumble of the coach.

The shotgunner turned to look at Reuben. "How come you know about that?"

"We met up with Tall Bull, traded for the girls and brought 'em home."

"Well, I'll be keelhauled and hung up to dry! If that don't beat all!" replied the shotgunner, shaking his head. "Whatchu think 'bout that, Whiskers?" nudging the driver.

"Ain't never heard of a Dog Soldier givin' up a captive!"

"Wal, you have now!"

"What'd you hafta trade?" asked the driver, looking over his shoulder at Reuben.

"Oh, a rifle, a knife and a hatchet, and his life."

"His life? You mean Tall Bull's life?"

"Ummhmm. He knew my wife had her rifle on him and if he didn't mind his manners, she woulda shot him. 'Course he didn't know she was a woman; he thought it was another man, but it still worked."

The shotgunner twisted around in his seat to look at the curled-up form of Elly, snuggled down among the baggage and bouncing along atop but snoozing all the while. He looked at Reuben. "That little bitty thing?"

"Ummhmm," answered Reuben, grinning.

After a brief stop at Dennison's ranch for a new team, the coach rocked out of the ranch and headed for Valley station where they would stop for a meal and allow some passengers to stay the night and perhaps take on others. When they pulled into Valley station, Reuben was surprised to see the larger station with two log buildings, a big barn and stable, other outbuildings and a large corral with at least fifty mules and horses. They had no sooner stopped and heard the announcement from the shotgunner about the meal and layover for some, than the east-bound stage rolled into the stop.

But it was an unannounced stop for the east bound as the shotgunner who would normally sound the bugle to let the hostlers know they were approaching, was unable to do much of anything. He had been shot and the front of his shirt was covered with blood, and he lay unconscious beside the driver who hollered at Reuben, "Here there, young man, help me with this man. He's wounded!"

Reuben quickly stepped up on the hub of the wheel, putting the other foot atop the wheel as he reached up to help the man to the ground. The shotgunner from their stage stood on the ground beside the wheel and reached up to take the unconscious man from Reuben. The driver said, "We was lucky, had a sawbones aboard and he bandaged him up some, said he'd work on the wound and try to get the bullet out when we stopped. Take him inside!" ordered the Jehu. Reuben asked the man, "What happened?"

"We got hit by three road agents the other side of Kelly's! They got the shipment from the bank in Denver, but 'twernt much, just one bag. They couldn't help him at Kelly's, so we come on to here. They got more room and can put him up."

Reuben helped the shotgunner get the man inside and noticed four men that had been sitting on the porch of the stage station, go to their horses and mount up to leave. He did not think much of it and helped the wounded man inside where they were directed to a back room and were followed by the man who called himself a doctor. He was a white-haired man, not much bigger than Elly, wearing a rumpled jacket over corded trousers, a dingy white shirt with a string tie and shoes that were down in the heel. He carried a tattered leather bag and directed the men with a wave of his hand and ordered the shotgunner, "Get me a bottle of whiskey and be quick about it!"

He waved Reuben away after they lay the man on the bed in the back room, and Reuben went to the main room to join Elly as she sat at the long table, two tin plates of food before her and a broad smile to welcome her man. "What was that all about?"

"The east-bound stage was hit by a band of outlaws who stole the bank's bag, wounded the shotgunner, and made their escape. The driver said the shotgunner might have winged one of the men with his shotgun, but he's not sure. It happened between Kelly's and Beaver Creek."

Elly nodded, lowered her voice so only Reuben could hear, "It might be nothing, but those men that were on the porch, well they got a message over the telegraph, read it, nodded to one another, and left. You might try to get something out of the telegrapher about what was in the message."

Reuben nodded, seated himself beside Elly and began on his meal of biscuits, beans, and bacon. He chuckled. "They must all have the same provisions, this ain't no different than the last stop," nodding at the plate.

Elly grinned. "Yeah, makes you hungry for some campfire deer steaks, don't it?"

"Ummhmm."

"We staying here or going on?" asked Elly.

"Let's keep goin'. The shotgunner, Levi, said Beaver Creek is a bit better, but we could just keep goin'. We'll decide after we get to Beaver Creek."

Elly chuckled. "I've been sleeping most of the way, so..." she shrugged, smiling at her man.

"I've noticed, but that's alright. You're cute when you're curled up," replied Reuben, grinning at his bride.

"Why thank you, sweetheart. That's plumb nice of you, it is," she said as she scooted closer to her man.

The telegrapher wasn't too keen on the idea of telling Reuben what was in the message to the men that left, but after Rueben scooted a twenty-dollar gold piece across the counter, the man looked around, grinned and pocketed the coin. He handed a copy of the gram to Reuben and turned away, returning to his key without another word.

Reuben waited until the coach was pulling out before he leaned back beside Elly and read the telegram, "Letter comin' from Ma. Pick her up Thursday at brother Crocket's place." It was signed, "Faraday".

They looked to one another, frowning, until Elly asked, "We'll need to find out about shipments, see if something is going out Thursday and then figure out where they're talking about. Brother Crocket's place? Must be some kinda code."

"Ummhmm, I'll see what I can find out without lettin'

anyone know what's up," replied Reuben, stuffing the paper in his pocket as he turned around. He caught movement on the low hills to the left, shaded his eyes to look, and tapped Levi, the shotgunner, on the shoulder to point out what he saw. "Looks like several riders comin' off the hills yonder, might be trouble!"

The sun was lowering quartered away to the north from their route. Reuben had retrieved his binoculars from his haversack and lifted them for a look at the riders to the south. "If you could hold this thing still, maybe I could get a better look," he spoke as he was jostled about atop the coach. He twisted around, bringing his knees up to give some stability as he lay his elbows on them, cradling the glasses against his face. The coach bounced into a rut, slamming the glasses against his face, and causing an outburst, "Hey!" He shook his head, rubbing his right eye and mumbled, "That's prob'ly gonna be black in the mornin'." He raised the glasses again, but sneaked a peek at the road, then snatched a quick look at the riders.

"There's 'bout twenty of 'em, but I don't see any war shields and none carryin' lances. No paint either. Maybe they're friendly," he suggested as he lowered the glasses. Elly lay his Sharps across his lap, nodding toward the riders. "Maybe we can just act like we don't see 'em till they make a move," he suggested.

Levi turned to look at Reuben. "Ever been in a Injun fight?"

"A time or two," he answered, checking the load on the Sharps. He had attached the telescopic sight, but with it being a side mount, he could use either the ladder sight or the scope. He looked toward the riders, watching as they rode down the slope of the low hill, but they showed no sign of trying to intercept the coach.

"The sight of any Injun makes me plumb nervous," declared the shotgunner, lifting his shotgun from beside him to stand it on his leg, keeping the pistol grip tight. He looked at the riders, and spoke over his shoulder to Reuben, "Can you tell what tribe they is?"

"Not sure, maybe Arapaho." He glanced to Elly who had brought her Henry from behind her and lay it across her lap, forcing a smile as she looked at Reuben. They had passed Godfrey's ranch without stopping and were making for Kelly's, also known as the American Ranch, but they were still two or three miles out.

"We ain't got fer to go to Kelly's!" declared Levi, reaching for his bugle to announce their arrival. "But it's still a ways," he shook his head, twisting to look at the riders. "Shore don't wanna bring all them Injuns down on the station, but we ain't enuff to fight 'em!"

Reuben lifted his field glasses for another look. "Looks like they stopped, maybe they're turnin' away," offered Reuben. He glanced at the road, hoping for a smooth stretch for a better look, lifted the glasses again and watched the riders. "Yeah, they're not comin' after us." He chuckled as he lowered the glasses, glancing from Elly to Levi and the Jehu. "Somebody must be livin' right," he chuckled, letting a nervous laugh escape.

"Ya don't reckon they'll wait'll we pass Kelly's?" asked Levi, looking to the driver.

Whiskers shook his head. "Dunno, which way'd they go?"

"They turned to the northeast, maybe just huntin', but they're not goin' the same way we are, and that suits me," declared Reuben.

"Me too. We'll make a switch at Kelly's, then skedaddle on to Beaver Creek. Beaver's a home station and the end of the line for us!" determined Whiskers.

"But will the stage continue?" asked Elly.

"Yup, but with another driver and shotgun," answered Whiskers, slapping the lines to the tired mules, coaxing a little more from the weary beasts.

AS THEY LEFT KELLY'S, A FRESH TEAM OF MULES LEANING into their traces, the sun split the low-lying clouds and sent golden lances heavenward and down into the flats. The golden orb turned orange with crimson edges as it settled behind the dark clouds. But the setting sun was not to be so soon forgotten as it lit the cloud afire and let the blaze of red spread across the low horizon. The stage rocked with the ruts in the road, the complaining passengers now silent with unanswered protests bitter in their mouths. The fifteen miles between Kelly's and the Beaver Creek station should be covered in less than two hours. That would mean they would arrive on the skirts of dusk, but the driver, Whiskers, picked up the pace as he lay out his blacksnake bullwhip, cracking it above the long ears of the mules and startling the animals to dig a little deeper and quicken their step. He glanced to his partner. "Well, I'm tired, an' I wanna go to bed! And I don't mean no dirt nap compliments of some Injun!" he growled, shaking his head and slapping the lines. The mules had broken into a canter and the stage rocked enough to render thoughts of anything but sleep.

Elly slapped Reuben on the shoulder and pointed to the south. A handful of riders had slipped from a shallow gulch and started toward the stage. There was no mistaking they were natives, and their intent was to overtake the stage, and whatever else they had in mind was open to question with no answers. Reuben motioned to their bundle for the Spencer, but he kept a tight hold on the Sharps. Elly nudged the shotgunner and pointed, and his first glance told the story. "Them Injuns is back!" he declared to the driver, motioning to the far left in the dim light of early dusk.

Elly shouted, "More on the right!"

Reuben had replaced the field glasses with the Sharps and was drawing a bead on the first bunch. He guessed them to be about six hundred yards away and he quickly adjusted the ladder sight. With the sight picture as steady as it could be, he squeezed off his first shot. The big blast of the Sharps startled both the driver and the shotgunner with the driver dropping his head into his shoulders and he hollered, "Yo mules! Git a move on you lazy lop-eared critters!"

Levi had turned to look at Reuben, then quickly looked where he had shot. A riderless horse had split off from the others, leaving a pile of buckskin and feathers behind. The others slowed their chase, looking back at their leader, now crumpled in the dirt and unmoving. They began shouting and gesturing until the Sharps bucked again and the portable cannon spat another big slug of lead that dropped the second warrior. The others shouted and quickly reined away from the far shooting rifle.

But those that were coming from the river side of

the trail burst from the tree line and charged through the greasewood and sage toward the stage road. Elly had bellied down atop the stage and brought her Henry up, aimed toward the charging warriors. The Henry blasted, bucked, and shoved against the small shoulder of the blonde, but the bullet flew true and the leader, a screaming warrior brandishing a scalplock decorated war lance, hunched over and slid backwards off his horse, landing in the same position, blood squirting from his throat. The man's head bounced once before the chin rested on his chest and he slowly fell to the side.

But Elly did not watch the first warrior; she was already taking aim on the second and dropped the hammer, almost simultaneously with Reuben squeezing off the first shot from the Spencer. The big bark of the Spencer masked the blast of the Henry, but one horse tripped and somersaulted, sending his rider twisting through the air to land on his neck and probably break his spine. Another horse bent in the middle, not because it was hit, but the rider had taken the slug in his chest and jerked back on the rein, forcing the horse to tumble to the ground, rolling on top of the rider and kicking his way free to run off toward the trees.

Whiskers had kicked the team to a full gallop and the long ears were laying back along the necks of each mule. They were digging deep and dragging the resistant coach into the dim light, regardless of the darkness they still stayed true to the road until Levi slapped Whiskers on the shoulder, "You can pull 'em in now," he hollered. "Injuns are all gone!"

Whiskers looked around, searching for any riders but there were none to be seen. He leaned back, pulling the ribbons tight, slowing the animals to a walk. The roar

71

and rattle of the creaking coach now almost silenced as Whiskers asked, "What happened?"

"Darndest thing I ever did see! Them two," pointing with his thumb over his shoulder, "done dropped four or five of 'em 'fore they got close 'nuff to do anything. Then the rest of 'em just made a caterwauling howl, tucked their tails and took off like a scalped porcupine!"

Whiskers looked at his partner, frowning. "You ever scalp a porcupine?"

"Wal, no, but'chu know what I mean!"

"As long as them Injuns are gone, it don't matter none to me if you wanna skin ever porcupine in the woods!"

"Now, why'd I wanna do a thing like that?" asked Levi, scooting his hat back on his head to scratch his scalp.

The trees beside the Platte River stood as silent shadows, cottonwoods standing above the willows and alder, chokecherry holding a skirt of darkness at ground level. The full moon showed its color as it slowly rose above the eastern horizon at their backs, but the light was welcomed as they rode into the darkness. Within moments, silence lay over the land, broken only by the rattle of trace chains, the moan of the rocking coach, and the clatter of harness, hames, and single trees as the mules plodded in the sandy soil at their feet.

Whiskers just shook his head, chuckling to himself, and slapped the lines on the mules, just to let them know he was still there and still in charge. Levi picked up the bugle and let it blow, although still about a half-mile away, it just felt better to let folks know they were still there and still kicking. Whiskers nodded to the golden west. "That there's the first look you'll get o' them Rockies! That big 'un stickin' its head in the clouds is Long's Peak."

Elly and Reuben shaded their eyes for a long first look at the sawtooth horizon, backlit by the setting sun that cast long lances of gold and orange across the darkening sky. The few remaining clouds caught the color with their rumpled bellies and lay like puffy quilts made by a loving grandma that used every bit of bright scrap she had in the home, making memories from the past, sewing hopes for the future. The stage rocked with the ruts, the bugle sounded its alarm, and hostlers came from the barn to snag the mules and help bring them to a stop. The dust cloud enveloped the crew and billowed over the top of the stage, prompting those atop to cover their faces with their neckerchiefs and fan the dust away as they coughed up the mud from the corners of their mouths.

Beaver Creek was a home station with two cabins, both with two rooms. One held the makeshift kitchen and dining table, while the second room had three sets of bunks, three high, with straw mattresses for the passengers willing to pay. Reuben and Elly opted to take to the loft in the barn, preferring the smell of horses and mules to the stench of unbathed men that had been eating beans all day.

As they rolled out their blankets, Elly spoke quietly, thinking back on their last few days, "You know, that was awful nice of Sadie and Mabel to let us have the reward on those men."

"Ummhmm, but they're happy they have a future now, and if we hadn't happened along, they'd be cookin' dog over some Cheyenne cookfire about now, if they had lived long enough."

"Well, they were happy with their share of the reward for the gold shipment return. With a little more'n a hundred dollars, that's probably the most money they've seen in a long time, if ever! And since they bought those dresses for the dance, I think the Cash brothers were happy also."

"There ya go again. You just can't help it, can you? Or is that just somethin' all women do?"

"What do you mean?" implored Elly, frowning at her man.

"Always tryin' to get folks married off! Jeremiah's happy about it, but Dustan, well, he's a little riled up, says he's too young."

"That's what he said after the dance, but when he walked her back to the hotel, he was whistling a different tune. I imagine, if we ever get back that way, they'll all be getting married soon."

Reuben stepped closer to his bride, took her in his arms. "I'm not concerned about them. We are already married, and I'm mighty happy about that!" He drew her close and they embraced, enjoying the moment of quiet and intimacy, moments that were getting hard to find.

11 / INVESTIGATING

"**P**romise me we won't take the stage back to Julesburg?" pleaded Elly, arching her back against the pain from bouncing on top the coach all day.

"No, I think we'll just get some horses and make our own way back. 'Sides, I want to look for any sign along the way of the highwaymen," replied Reuben as he gathered their gear. Like before at Beaver Creek, Latham was a home station, and they would spend the night and take a different coach on into Denver City. The day had been a long one, but uneventful with team changes at Junction, Bijou Creek, a meal stop at Fremont's Orchard, another change at Eagle's Nest and the day of travel ended at Latham.

Latham was a busier station than most, situated at the confluence of the Cache la Poudre and South Platte Rivers, it was also the way station where the coach lines split, one going north to cross the mountains at the North Platte Crossing and on to Fort Bridger, eventually making its way to California, and the other back the way they came to Julesburg and the east. Reuben and Elly

75

stacked their gear just inside the barn and walked around the station for a much needed stretch of the legs.

"This is the busiest stop we've seen," noted Elly, nodding to four wagons that pulled in near the barn. The two-story station offered lodging for the night, with preferential treatment for stage passengers, and a makeshift restaurant serving family style and charging one dollar per head per meal. Reuben nodded to several saddle horses tied at the hitch rail. "Looks like they get other customers also," he stepped closer to the horses, noted the lather dried at the girth and across the chests under the martingale. "Those horses have been ridden hard. And their riders seemed to be more concerned with themselves than their horses. Any man that appreciates his horse would always tend to the animal before himself, makin' sure they were fed and watered and rubbed down should always be a priority."

"What's it to you?!" growled a grizzled man who stepped from the doorway, posturing on the stoop, and glaring at Reuben. His thumbs stuffed into his belt as he hitched his britches up and coughed, wiping his mouth on his already dirtied sleeve.

Reuben frowned, looked at the man. "I just know horseflesh and it's easy to see when an animal is abused, like that one," nodding to the black at the rail.

"That's my horse and I'll do with him how I see fit! And ain't nuthin' you can do about it, pilgrim!" growled the man, stepping closer. He was the same height as Reuben, barrel chested, whiskers that obscured his face and seemed to blend with his hair and eyebrows, leaving slits for his eyes. Tobacco juice stained the chin whiskers, and the remains of his last few meals decorated the rest. When he growled, he showed a mouth full of rotten teeth, and the stench of his unwashed body wafted from the stoop and overshadowed the smell of lathered horses.

Elly tugged at Reuben's sleeve, whispered, "C'mon, he ain't worth it!"

"Yeah, do what the little filly says," snickered the man, "'fore I whup you proper, stomp you into the ground, and take that little filly to the barn to show her what a real man is!"

Reuben took one step away, dropped his arm from Elly's grip, and brought his fist from below his knee as he pivoted on the ball of his foot and buried the hammer like fist in the belly of the filthy beast. The man's eyes flared, his mouth opened, as he bent in the middle, staggering forward off the two steps of the stoop, but Reuben stepped to the side, clasped his fists together and brought them down like an axe on the back of the man's neck, dropping him to the ground in a clump. The man struggled for breath, but Reuben and Elly walked away as if nothing happened.

They walked to the second of the two buildings, a one-story that served more as the stage station and telegraph office, leaving the eating, drinking, and sleeping to the main building. Reuben and Elly stepped into the room, the gold from the setting sun bending through the windows to show one man busy at the telegraph key. The shelf above the desk was loaded with the large batteries, all linked with wires and such, and the man, bald with a friar's ring just above his ears, garters on his sleeves, sat with one ear cocked toward the rattling apparatus and his hand busy writing his decipher.

They went to the counter, watching the man busy at his work and when the key silenced and he finished his writing, Reuben said, "Excuse me!" startling the man so much he bounced in his chair as he turned to scowl at the intrusion.

"Skeert me!" declared the man, shaking his head and chuckling as he stood. "So, what can I help you with?"

Reuben withdrew the copy of the telegram given him by the telegrapher at Valley Station, flattened it on the counter and pushed it to the man who doubled as the clerk for the station. "Did you send this to Valley Station?"

The little man looked at it, scowled. "Was this sent to you?"

"No, but it did go to the Valley Station."

"Then you shouldn't have a copy of it! That's private!" whined the little man, shaking the paper before him like a witch's wand, trying to make Reuben disappear.

Reuben stood tall, looked around the empty room and leaned on the counter. "Look, we believe this was sent by or to the men that have robbed the gold shipments from the stage. We think they're workin' with the Confederates out of Mace's Hole, and we need to know who sent it and where they might be or if they are expected to return." He tried to look as conspiratorial as possible, hoping to let the little man think he could help the company and stop the holdups.

"Well, well," he stammered as he looked at the missive again, "Yes, it was sent from here. I remember because the man that sent it did not look like he had a mother! See here," and he pointed at the text of the message, "he signed his name Faraday, but the other men called him 'Stink' which certainly suited him. And here, where it says brother Crocket's, one of the men with Stink was called Crocket. So, it didn't make any sense to me, but I sent it."

"Would you recognize the man if he came in again?" asked Reuben.

"Of course. I would recognize him by his smell if nothing else, but he hangs around here off and on, him and his cohorts, sends and receives grams more'n anybody. Ain't never seen the like. I saw him today and he sent another telegram but it went back to Denver." He sorted through his papers, found the gram and lay it on the counter before Reuben. "There, that's the one."

The message was sent to Faraday in Denver, *Farm burned by Indians, cousins dead, lost everything.* Crocket.

"See there, the same one that signed it Faraday, now sent one to Faraday and signed it Crocket. I thought there was something wrong with that, but I didn't know what," declared the clerk, stepping back with one hand on his hip and a smug expression covering his face as he looked down past his spectacles that sat on the end of the turned-up nose.

"Well, thank you, uh," started Reuben until the man interjected.

"Ferdinand, Ferdinand McGee."

"Yes, Ferdinand. But if these men come back, do not act like you suspect anythin'. These are dangerous men and not to be crossed. My name is Reuben Grundy, and I will check back with you either in person, or by telegram. So, keep track of what they send, and that will help us apprehend them, and maybe get you a share in any reward!"

"Reward?" asked the surprised clerk.

"Yes, the stage company quite often gives rewards to those that help apprehend the highwaymen."

"Oh, my, that would be wonderful!" declared the man, smiling and twisting around as if he were on a dance floor.

Reuben frowned, looked at Elly with one eyebrow raised, and motioned to the door where they quickly took their leave. Elly giggled, looked at Reuben. "For a moment there, I thought you were going to tell him you were a deputy marshal."

"I'm not even used to the idea myself, so I'm not about to tell somebody else. But I think we are gettin' a pretty good idea as to how they're able to just hit the coaches carryin' gold. There's somebody, this Faraday, in Denver that puts 'em onto the right stage."

"So, what do we do now?"

"We'll go on into Denver City, talk to the telegrapher there, see if we can find out how they know the gold's goin' out, and maybe get the culprit there. Other'n that, I dunno. I'm kinda new at this investigatin' stuff."

Elly giggled. "Me too!" as they started to the main building to get something to eat.

"There he is!" shouted the man that tried to take down Reuben before. Behind him stood two other men, each as scruffy as the first and bearing a little resemblance to the first man. Reuben stepped forward, nudging Elly behind him, and faced the new threat.

"You again? I thought you'd learned your lesson, but if you want more," and he turned a little sideways to the man, his left shoulder forward as he gave the man the 'come-on' signal with his hand, grinning all the while. "Couldn't do it alone, huh? Had to get your ugly brothers to help you out?" chided Reuben.

"Don't need no help fer the likes o' you. And like I said 'fore, I'm gonna take your woman when I'm done with you," he cackled as he charged, arms outstretched. He had probably used that move before, usually on smaller men, hoping to get them in a bear hug and snap their ribs as he used his big arms to squeeze the life out of his prey.

Reuben chuckled as the man charged, making the man frown at his response. He was used to other men ducking and running, or showing so much fear they froze in place, but this man was laughing at him. Reuben ducked under his arm, brought up his knee to the man's groin and drove his elbow into the man's ribs as he stumbled and fell on his face, grabbing his crotch in pain. He moaned, twisting to the side, looked at his friends, and said, "Git him!"

But before they took a step, they were staring down the muzzles of two pistols, Reuben's and Elly's, and both were smiling with a wicked smile as Elly said, "Come on boys, do as your friend says. This little ol' pistol and it's .36 caliber bullet won't hurt *too* much, except when it blows out the back of your skull!"

Reuben glanced at his woman, saw her expression, and looked at the two men, standing frozen with their arms outstretched and hands empty. "You might want to re-think that fellas, I think she's pretty serious," as he nodded to Elly.

The two men carefully stepped back, glancing from their fallen friend to the two with pistols, shrugging as they saw the expression on their friend's face. "We cain't do nuthin', Stink."

The man on the ground growled as he rolled to his side and struggled to get to his feet. Reuben looked at the man, saw his expression, and said, "If you want to chance it, come on. But know this is a Remington Army and it packs a wallop, and I can pull the trigger faster'n you fellas can move. I suggest you just get on your worn-out horses and find someplace else to cause trouble."

"This ain't over," growled the brute of a leader.

"It better be, if you know what's good for you, and tell your friend Crocket," nodding to the man behind him, "to mind his manners also."

They watched as the three went to their horses and swung aboard, trying to cast looks back to Reuben and Elly, but the two still stood with pistols cocked and aimed, waiting for the trio to disappear.

A different coach, the driver known as Whip and the shotgunner called Windy, took little convincing to let Reuben and Elly ride up top. Elly had arranged their gear and other baggage to make a comfortable seat for herself as Reuben rode behind the driver and shotgunner. He struck up a conversation with the two, "You two ever been drivin' when the stage was robbed?"

Windy twisted around to look at Reuben, suspicion showing in his eyes. "Why?"

"Just wonderin'. I've heard tell of different robberies and attacks by Indians, and kinda wanted to know what me and the missus would be in for," explained Reuben. "We were hit by some Indians the other side of Beaver Creek, but it didn't amount to much."

"Say, are you the two that Levi was talkin' about what kilt all them Injuns?" asked Whip, glancing over his shoulder at Reuben.

"Oh, we helped out a bit, is all," answered Reuben.

"Well, mighty glad to have you aboard, although we don't 'spect no trouble down thisaway. What with some

83

sojers at Fort Lupton and such, don't reckon any Injuns'll try anythin'."

"What about highwaymen?"

"Now there's no tellin' 'bout that sort. Sometimes ain't no more'n a drunk cowboy an' his friends wantin' to get 'nuff for a night on the town, other times, wal there's some what gets purty serious 'bout their work, dangerous too." He slapped the stock of his shotgun he kept across his lap, "But I got my faithful friend Myrtle, here, and she's a match for anybody!"

Reuben chuckled. "I bet she is!"

They switched teams at Big Bend, six strong draft horses took to the trail as an old friend. The big horses liked the trail, enjoying the freedom and opportunity to stretch their legs, the leaders often anxious to pick up the pace. "So, I noticed the teams since Fremont's Orchard have been horses, no mules. What's the reason for that?" asked Reuben.

"Ah, they use the mules 'tween the orchard and Julesburg cuz o' the deep sand. The mules do a better job o' pullin' in the soft soil. But when we're on good ground, these horses like to stretch out and make time," explained Windy. He pointed to the side. "That there's what remains of Fort St. Vrain, lotta history there 'bout the early days, trappers an' such." He paused reflecting on the history. "Little further on, we'll pass the site of Fort Vasquez, it's pretty much all gone too."

"I s'pose next you're gonna be tellin' how you was a trapper an' traded with Vasquez," prodded the driver, chuckling.

"Nope, but muh daddy was! He told many a tale 'bout his life in the mountains 'fore he came home to momma an' me. Rough life it were, yessir."

Their stop at Fort Lupton was a short stop for a meal and they were soon back on the trail, bound for Pierson's Station, about fifteen miles further south, another swing station for a change of team before pressing on to Denver City. The stage line road sided the South Platte all the way to the confluence with Cherry Creek, although not the site of the first gold find, it was the site of most of the town and the supply hub for the Colorado Gold Rush.

But it did little to resemble a supply hub when the coach rolled into the town. Reuben and Elly were looking around at a scene of destruction and desolation. Everywhere they looked, rubble from some massive fire stood like blackened skeletons of what had been a bustling town. Although there were many crews busy with clean-up, their faces and arms blackened with soot, others had already started rebuilding. The foundations of buildings were showing as bricklayers busied themselves building bigger and better buildings for Denver City businesses.

The coach pulled up beside a white clapboard, two-story building with a sign, *Planter's House Hotel* and another smaller sign, *Overland Stage Line*. Two hostlers had grabbed the bridles and bits of the leaders, holding them steady while the passengers stepped down and two station workers unloaded the baggage and mail pouches. The coach would undergo a once over and clean-up before putting it back into use, probably on a return run to Julesburg.

Reuben and Elly walked into the station, then ducked through the doorway to the Planter House desk to secure a room. Reuben was fortunate to get the last room available, "You are a mighty fortunate man, sir. That room was just vacated, and all the rooms are in great demand, what with the fire and all," stated the clerk as he handed the key to Reuben.

"Thank you," stated Reuben, looking at the key and number, "Second floor?" he asked.

"Yessir, all the way to the end. There is an outside stairway if that would be more convenient for you sir."

"Thank you, it would. And where is the nearest livery?"

"Do you wish to rent a carriage sir?"

"Maybe, but I might also be lookin' to buy a horse or two."

"Very good, sir," began the clerk, then gave Reuben directions to the livery and added, "Also, there is a good ranch just south of here about five or six miles that has excellent horses. You might want to try there. It's the Applegate ranch."

"Thank you again, you're very helpful," declared Reuben. He turned to Elly, handed her the key. "Maybe you would like to go to the room while I get our gear?"

Elly smiled, looked at the clerk. "A bath?" she asked.

"Yes, ma'am, the room for baths is two doors down from your room. Would you like me to have the help prepare one for you?"

"Yes, please. And where will I find a dressmaker's shop?"

Again, he gave directions and summoned the help to prepare a bath for the lady, even as he glanced sideways with one eyebrow raised, at the description of the woman attired like an Indian woman as a lady.

Since the fire, the stage station doubled as the telegraph office, and Reuben stopped by the telegrapher's counter to ask a few questions. When the clerk stood before him, Reuben asked, "I spoke with the telegrapher in Latham, and he happened to mention a telegram he sent to a Faraday. Now, I had a friend in the army, a captain Faraday. You don't suppose they're one and the same, do you?"

The man looked at Reuben with an expression of disdain, frowning at the intruder to his domain. "Now, how would I know that?" he asked, shaking his head at what he thought was a less than intelligent suggestion.

"Well, he's a big guy, taller'n me, brown wavy hair, clean-shaven, and well dressed, like you'd expect a former military man to be," explained Reuben as he pulled some folded greenbacks from his pocket and began peeling off a few.

"I have seen no such person," declared the man, watching Reuben's toying with the greenbacks, "however, there was a man, in uniform, an officer but I don't know what rank, and he called himself Faraday. He was my height, lean, well-trimmed chin whiskers, and distinguished looking. The grams he sent were regarding his mother, apparently, she has been ill, and the Indians destroyed their farm. He's been worried about her and has sent messages back and forth to his brothers, I believe."

"That could be him. Do you think he'll be back in?" asked Reuben. "I'd sure like to catch up to him."

"I believe he will be back; he still has not completed arrangements to get his mother here."

Reuben reached over the counter, offering his hand to shake. "Thank you sir! You've been a big help. By the way if you see him again, would you send word to my room, 218? But don't say anythin' to him, I'd like it to be a surprise." He pushed a ten-dollar greenback across the counter, smiling at the man whose eyes flared as he reached for the bill.

"Happy to be of service, sir."

IT TOOK TWO TRIPS TO PACK EVERYTHING UP THE BACK stairs and Elly left the room door open for him, waving over her shoulder as she started to the bathroom. She smiled coyly over her shoulder and said, "I'll make sure they get one ready for you after I'm done!"

Although most stores were closed by the time they settled in, they had some fresh duds in their gear, and they donned them to go to supper in the Planters House restaurant. Reuben wore his dark green uniform trousers with his plaid shirt tucked in, while Elly donned her split skirt made for her in Julesburg. Her gingham top with lace around the collar set off her blonde hair and she smiled at her husband as they sat at the corner of the table, joining hands under the table. The waitress took their order and within a few moments, she returned with two big plates overflowing with delectable items. Each plate bore a juicy beef steak partially covered with potatoes and gravy, carrots and asparagus were covered with fresh butter and sat at the edge of the plates. Steaming coffee was set beside the plates and the waitress asked, "Will there be anything else?"

Reuben looked from his plate to Elly and back to the waitress. "Might want some pie after we're done with all this!" he declared, smiling at the matronly woman who stood with hands on her hips and a smile splitting her face. She nodded and turned away, disappearing into the kitchen.

Elly looked at Reuben. "You know, this meal might make the last few days bouncing on that stage worthwhile!" and smiled broadly as she picked up her knife and fork to go to work on the meal, but Reuben held up his hand, frowned, and lowered his eyes and bent his head. He reached for her hand and quietly began to say thanks to the Lord for His safety, provision, and protection. He finished with, "And Lord, help me to get on the outside of all this and still have room for that pie! Thank you, Lord, Amen!"

13 /SOUTH

Crocket

    Come home stop Arrangements to be made for Mother's funeral.

    Faraday.

"That's all he said, honest. And he wasn't upset or nuthin'. You'd think a man that lost his mother would be a little sad, but he looked almost happy. Then he went into the dining room, yonder. I think he's still there!" declared the telegrapher. He had sent word to Reuben about the man calling himself Faraday as requested.

"Thank you, sir," replied Reuben, pulling the copy of the telegram closer, as he pushed the five-dollar greenback across the counter under his palm.

The clerk slipped it into his vest pocket, nodding and smiling. "Will there be anything else, sir?"

"Only if he sends any more messages. Now, tell me, did this just go to Latham or...?"

"Oh, just to Latham. Although before he would send the same message to Valley Station, but not this time. It might be because of the last message he received that told of the Indian attack and the death of the cousins."

Reuben glanced up at the clerk, he frowned at the thought and the realization that the cousins' death might have been the four outlaws that had the gold shipment, who he and the girls had put in the ground. *So, maybe they are connected.* "And you say he's in the dinin' room?"

"Yessir, you won't miss him, he's in his usual uniform, and he walks mighty proud."

"Thanks again," he paused, frowning, "say, what is your name, anyway?"

The clerk chuckled, "Smith, sir, Henry J. Smith."

"Very good, Henry. We'll keep this to ourselves?"

"Oh, yessir!"

Reuben joined Elly in the foyer and as they started for the dining room, they were intercepted by Whip and Windy. "Wal, if'n it ain't the great Injun fighters! Howdy folks!" declared Windy, always the more talkative of the two. "Goin' to the dinin' room are ye?"

"Ummhmm, and you?" asked Reuben.

"Positively! I'm so hungry my stomach thinks muh throat's been cut, and it's been growlin' at me all mornin' protestin' the fact. So, hows 'bout you two joinin' us for breakfast? Whip's buyin'!"

"We'd be happy to, Windy," replied Elly, taking his arm with her free hand. With Reuben on one side, Windy on the other, and led by Whip, the four entered the dining room and quickly found a table by the window, somewhat apart from the rest of the diners. Reuben glanced around and spotted the man Faraday, saw he was with another man who looked like a local businessman, and noticed they were seated apart from the others and appeared to be speaking in low tones, often glancing around at others in the room.

As they were seated, Reuben noticed Whip had a folded-up newspaper, somewhat dog-eared and tattered, and he asked Whip, "So, what's new with the war?"

"Hummph, nothin' much, not since that stand-off 'tween Lee and McClellan at Antietam last fall. And after Lincoln issued his Emancipation Proclamation makin' all them coloreds free men, well, can't say much has happened, but mark my words, it's goin' to!" growled the usually cheerful Whip.

"No, I mean here in the territory? What's new hereabouts?" asked Reuben.

"Oh, oh, well, that's different." He chuckled. "After that run-in last spring down at Glorieta Pass, them southerners tucked their tails and skedaddled outa here! Ain't really been no battles here in Colorado territory, although from what I hear, there's plenty o' them southern sympathizers." He leaned forward and lowered his voice, "The Second Colorado Infantry, Captain Theodore H. Dodd, commanding, is a unit put together from volunteers down round Cañon City. They rousted out that bunch from Mace's Hole this spring, sent 'em all packin' 'ceptin' for forty some odd they took prisoner." Whip leaned back smiling, nodding, then leaned forward again. "And two o' them prisoners were the Reynolds brothers, and some folks say he's the one whut set fire to Denver, bragged about goin' to do it, and they think he done it. But he's in jail now, yessiree!" Again he sat back, crossed his arms and nodded his head, grinning widely.

But their news gathering was interrupted by the waitress with a pot of steaming hot coffee who began filling their cups. When she filled the last, she stepped back and asked, "So, what'll you have?"

"What's the special?" asked Windy, looking around.

The waitress nodded to a small blackboard near the

entry way. "There it is, same as always. Eggs, steak, and taters."

"Then I reckon we'll have the special!"

"Good choice," she declared as she turned away.

Reuben looked at Whip. "So, how is it you know so much about what's goin' on?"

Whip chuckled, relaxed, and leaned forward again. "Cuz Cap'n Dodd is my son!" he declared proudly.

Windy leaned back, frowning. "You ain't never tol' me you had a son in the army!"

"You ain't never shut up long enough for me to tell you!"

"Well, I'll be..."

"Prob'ly," replied Whip, grinning.

Reuben thought about what Whip had revealed and asked, "Are you in regular touch with your son?"

"Ummhmm, he's in Denver City now, been o'er to the governor's place with some other officers, talkin' things over. You know how it is."

"You think I could meet him? I ain't never met a real live hero like that before," asked Reuben, trying his best to look overly interested and a little excited.

"Dunno. I will be seein' him this afternoon, sometime. He said he'd come and have supper with me 'fore he leaves to rejoin his unit. Maybe you could join us, you, and the missus?" he suggested, nodding to Elly, who smiled at the suggestion.

Reuben looked at Elly who smiled back, already reading a little of what he was thinking and with a simple nod she answered, "That would be nice, of course there is some business we have to tend to, horses, supplies, and more. What time should we meet with you, Whip?"

The whiskery driver dropped his eyes, a flush coming

to his face, and he stammered, "Oh, I'd say, 'bout dusk, ma'am. That'd be a good time, maybe you folks could get your business done and muh son'd be back in time. That suit?"

Elly looked at Reuben who nodded, and she answered for them, "That would be fine, Whip, wonderful. Now, how 'bout we finish up with this meal first 'fore we tie into the business for the day."

They made short work of the meal, but Reuben noticed the officer and his businessman friend appeared to finish their business and although the businessman stood to leave, the officer remained seated, and watched his friend start from the restaurant. Reuben leaned over to Elly and whispered, "I'm gonna see where that fella goes, I'm thinkin' they're up to somethin'. I'll be right back."

"Excuse me, gentlemen, I left somethin' in our room. I'll be right back," he explained as he rose from his seat, "If you'll watch over my fair lady till I return?"

"Why, of course! As long as it's alright with you, little missy?" replied Whip.

Elly smiled and nodded reaching for her coffee cup as Reuben stepped away from the table. He casually walked into the foyer just as the businessman exited the front door. With a couple strides taking him to the window, he pushed back the curtain to watch the man saunter across the street, turn back to look behind him, then take to the boardwalk toward the rebuilding of the big new brick bank building that housed the Clark, Gruber & Co., Bank and Mint. After the fire, most of the buildings were being rebuilt with stone and brick and the bank was setting the pace. A smaller frame structure stood to the front, a temporary office, while the larger structure was slowly rising behind. The man pushed his way through the front door and Reuben quickly followed.

When Reuben, still less than finely outfitted with his uniform trousers and buckskin tunic, stepped into the bank office, several eyes looked his direction, unimpressed. A quick glance showed the back of the man he followed disappearing through an office door with the name *R. J. Dinwoodie, VP* painted on the opaque glass. Reuben strolled to one of the teller cages and asked the clerk, "Was that Mr. Dinwoodie that just went in there?"

"Yessir. Did you have an appointment?"

"Uh, no, but I was referred to the bank here by Mr. Holladay. I have a draft here I would like to deposit and be able to draw on it for some purchases I plan to make. Would you handle that for me?" asked Reuben, reaching into his pocket for the reward draft given by the stage line.

"Oh, yessir, yessir. Your name sir?"

"It will be in the name of Reuben and Eleanor Grundy. And could you recommend a good haberdasher for some new clothes and a dressmaker for my wife?"

"Oh, yessir," jovially answered the teller and began to explain about a couple of businesses that would undoubtedly suit a discriminating buyer. "And on the corner is the largest general supply emporium, the Koch's."

Reuben was very casual as he tended his business and chuckled. "You know, when I followed Mr. Dinwoodie across the street, I was certain I heard him whistlin' Dixie, almost made me homesick. Isn't that a little odd for this part of the country?"

The teller glanced around, chuckling, smiled and spoke softly, "Oh no, sir. There are many around that came from the South and some have even flown the stars and bars over their business, but not so much anymore. Mr. Dinwoodie is from Alabama, but I'm sure his thoughts are not about the war now. He's moving up in the ranks of the banking business, yessir."

"Well, it's no concern of mine," replied Reuben, accepting the paperwork from the teller. "Thank you for your help, Mr..." he paused as he turned the nameplate around, "Mr. Hinsdale. Thank you."

"You're quite welcome, Mr. Grundy. And welcome to our fine bank. If there is anything we can do to assist you, please don't hesitate to ask. We are here to serve."

Reuben tipped his hat and turned away, a brief glance to the office of Dinwoodie, and quickly exited the bank to rejoin Elly to conduct their business for the day. He had already learned most of what he had suspected, now hopefully he could learn more from Whip's son before the next shipment was due to leave.

T he dining room of the Planters House was packed with the after-work crowd of businesspeople and tradesmen, although many tables were crowded with mixed couples. With the clatter of dishes, the hum of conversations, the shuffle of chairs and feet, it seemed alive with life. But with all the hubbub, most eyes turned to look at the handsome blond couple that entered the wide doorway and with a nod, pushed their way through the crowd to join the three men at the table by the window who stood, motioning to the entering couple.

Reuben and Elly were outfitted in their new duds and were similarly attired. While Elly had a well-tailored split skirt that reached her ankles with a full flare, topped with a ruffled white brocade cotton blouse, Reuben had fitted black trousers and a white linen shirt, and both had black leather frock style jackets. The jackets were of big horn ram skin with little adornment making them lightweight yet serviceable and appeared to be tailored for the two. Reuben carried his new flat crowned, rolled brim felt hat and had Elly's arm linked in his as they maneuvered through the crowd.

Elly greeted the three with a broad smile and a slight nod. "Gentlemen."

"Mrs. Grundy, this is my son, Captain Theodore H. Dodd, or as we call him, Teddy!" began a smiling Whip, grinning at his son.

Elly extended her hand to the captain, who gladly accepted it and nodded as he replied, "Pleased to make your acquaintance, Ma'am." He quickly looked to Reuben. "And you must be the Reuben that my father has told me about." He extended his hand to Reuben, who accepted it with a firm shake and replied, "I am. Pleased to meet you, Captain."

Reuben pulled out the chair for Elly, seated her as the men seated themselves, and sat beside her. He looked at the captain and began the conversation with, "So, your father tells me you led the troop that cleared out Mace's Hole of the confederates. Is that right?"

The captain dropped his eyes to the table, glanced at his father, and looked to Reuben. "It was my unit that had that duty, yes. But since then, it's been mostly scouting and patrolling. Not much happening this far west." He looked at Reuben. "My father said he thought you had served with the Union, is that right?"

Reuben nodded. "With Berdan's Sharpshooters, yes. I mustered out after takin' a couple pieces of lead in the chest."

"What brought you out west?"

"That's kind of a long story. Chasin' some raiders, some gun-runners, outlaws, and runnin' after this young lady," he explained, reaching for Elly's hand and giving her a big smile. He looked at the captain. "So, what's next for you and your troop, Captain?"

"Ted, please." He looked at his father, grinned. "Well, I

get to ride herd on my father for a few days coming up soon."

Whip turned to look at his son. "What's this? You're ridin' with us?"

"Well, not riding with you, just trailing along with you."

Whip and Windy both frowned, looking at the captain, but before they could say anything, the server stepped to their table to take their orders. Once she was done and turned away, Whip asked, "Why you gonna ride with us?"

"Well, as you know, there have been several stages robbed of their gold shipments and you'll be carrying a sizable load soon, so, my troop has been assigned the job of guarding the shipment."

Whip frowned, looking from his son to Windy and to Reuben, "Should you be talkin' 'bout that?"

The captain let a slow grin split his face as he glanced from his father to Reuben and Elly. He looked at his father. "You don't know, do you?"

"Know what?"

"Who these two are," with a slight nod to Reuben and Elly.

Whip frowned, looking from Windy to his son and to Reuben to see if they knew what he was talking about. He slowly shook his head as he answered, "Well, 'bout all I know is they are mighty handy to have around when the Injuns attack."

The captain leaned close to his Pa and whispered, "They are deputy marshals!"

Whip acted like he had been hit as he leaned back and looked at Reuben and Elly. "No, cain't be!"

The captain frowned, motioning him to be quiet, and

looked at Reuben who was also frowning. "The governor told me about you two and your appointment as marshals and that you were primarily assigned the task of protecting the stage lines. I didn't know I would meet you so soon, but I'm glad I did. Perhaps we can work together to plan the next shipment which will be delivered to the Stage Line office tomorrow." He spoke in low tones, his back to the crowded dining room and did his best to keep his flustered father from asking too many questions.

Reuben grinned. "No one knows about our bein' marshals. We've kept it to ourselves, and it has helped a little in the investigation. Perhaps after dinner we can go someplace a little more private and discuss the details, if that would be acceptable?"

"Of course, of course." He looked at his father, "Do you think we could use the office at the Stage Line Barn?"

"Sure," he replied, but their conversation was stayed by the arrival of the meal at their table.

Throughout the meal and the minimal conversation, Elly caught Whip and Windy both looking up at her and shaking their head, until she asked, "What is it, Whip?"

"What do you mean, Missy?"

"You keep looking at me and shaking your head, what's going on in that mind of yours?"

He shook his head again, took a long sip of steaming coffee, and answered, "I just can't figger you bein' a deputy marshal!"

Windy said, "After we seen her shoot them Injuns, I reckon she can be just about anythin' she wants!"

Both Elly and Reuben smiled, and Reuben added, "First time I saw her was when the Cheyenne Dog soldiers had captured her and a couple others. First chance she got she grabbed up a rifle and cut loose! Sent them Dog soldiers hightailin' it real quick like! It was then I figgered she was a woman to ride beside me!" He reached for her hand to give it a squeeze as she blushed at the comments.

"If that don't beat all!" declared Whip, wiping his whiskers and grinning.

"THERE'S GOING TO BE TWO CHESTS, EACH ABOUT A hundred pounds of gold bars from the Clark and company mint. That figures out to be about $100,000. And there will be more shipments later."

"Whooeee! We ain't never carried that much 'fore!" declared Windy, shaking his head.

They had opted for the small office in the livery, and it was a bit crowded with Reuben, Elly, Whip, Windy, the captain and the boss of the freighters, Henry Hatcher, a mountain of a man that stood close to six and a half feet tall and filled any doorway he could fit through. Captain Dodd nodded to Hatcher. "I asked Henry to join us since his freighters are a part of the plan." With another nod to Hatcher, the big man stepped forward. "We've got eight freighters that will head out in the mornin', four goin' north through Namaqua and Spring Creek, the rest of us goin' through Latham and on to Julesburg. We're carryin' supplies for the stations and won't be movin' as fast as the coaches."

As the big teamster paused, the captain added, "We will have four additional men, troopers in civilian clothes, that will ride with the freighters bound for Julesburg."

"But what's all this about the freighters have to do with us?" asked Windy, scratching his head as he listened to the explanations. "If'n we're carryin' the gold, seems to me we're the ones what need more men an' such."

The captain grinned and looked at Windy. "The rest of my troop will be following the stage, and there will be two additional men atop your coach. But there will be two chests of gold of gold and two chests of lead bars."

"Wal, now, you're really gettin' me confused!" drawled Windy as he dropped his eyes and scratched his thinning hair again.

Reuben had noticed Windy and his ways before and had begun to realize that although he put on a show of being a little slow on the uptake, he was not quite the backward man he showed himself. Whether it was just some means of self-preservation, or something more sinister remained to be seen, but Reuben was hopeful the man was as genuine as he appeared.

"Although the coach will have two chests," explained the captain, nodding to two chests stacked in the corner of the office, "and the freighters will have two chests, the only one that will know where the gold will be is the marshal here," explained the captain. "But as far as anybody else is concerned, they," nodding to Reuben and Elly, "have nothing to do with the shipment, or with the stage line or freighters. So, I suggest we all turn in because the gold will be brought here to the livery first thing in the morning."

" **G**eneral Sibley said we *must* stop any gold shipments to the Union!" declared Captain George Madison as he stood before the remnant of his confederate troops. The rag-tag bunch had been recruited from the few settlements in southern Colorado territory and were the last of those that had escaped the raid on Mace's Hole by the 1st Colorado Cavalry. The band of rebels numbered less than sixty men and were a detachment of Company A of Well's Texas Battalion under the command of General Douglas Cooper. Many of the men that escaped the raid on Mace's Hole had fled south to the Texas battalion and several had been reassigned to the Colorado detachment.

"Well, Captain, are we gonna strike in force or what?" asked First Sergeant Maxwell Hennesey, the senior ranking non-com of the company.

"My information is the gold will be shipped out on the Overland Stage tomorrow and will be going East to Philadelphia. This shipment will be $100,000 and they plan on more to follow, but General Sibley doesn't want any of it to get into Union hands. So my plan is to intercept the stage the day after tomorrow after it leaves Latham. According to the banker, there will be a small contingent of Union troops following the stage, but we can handle them with a diversion."

After the raid on Mace's Hole, the band of remaining confederates had gathered at their secondary location in the mountains by Turkey Creek, not far from Denver City or the gold fields to the south. Although mostly a hodge-podge gathering of committed sympathizers that had been away from the Hole when the raid happened, most were not much more than raw recruits, yet none were lacking in their zeal and desire to be a part of the confederacy. The captain turned to the man on his right, Lieutenant Isaac Washington, motioned him to the wall tent that served as their command post, looked to the rest of the men. "We leave in one hour. We'll be traveling mostly at night and will not be returning here anytime soon, so take what you need!" With nods and a few grumbles, the men dispersed to their bedrolls to ready their gear and their horses.

"Lieutenant," began the captain as he entered the tent, "you and your men will be responsible for the diversion. So between now and then, you need to pick out the best marksmen for your troop because you'll be staging an ambush and your first volley must cut the odds down, we won't be able to sustain a long battle. We have to hit hard and run."

"How many Union troops do you expect will be with the stage?" asked the green officer. He was a young man with little more than fuzz on his chin and a blend of excitement and fear in his eyes. His family was from Georgia and had come to the west in the first days of the gold rush, but his father had been killed in a rockslide in the mountains, leaving him to care for his mother and little sister. When his mother decided to return to Georgia, Isaiah had been listening to the rumors of war and thought it would be his opportunity to prove he was a man. Col. John Heffiner, the first commander of the fledgling confederate company in Colorado territory who had been commissioned by General Sibley to recruit men for the south in the early years of the war had recruited him to the confederate cause and because of his education, gave the young man a commission. Isaiah had missed every other opportunity to get in the fight and was determined to show himself capable.

"From what I can gather, they will have about the same number, one company. But you will go against them with half our force while the sergeant and I take the others against the stage to capture the gold. You will have to keep the troops pinned down or eliminated until we get the gold."

"You can count on us, Captain!" declared the young officer, his enthusiasm overcoming his first shock of fear.

"Then get your gear together, we move out in one hour!" ordered the captain with a glance to the seasoned sergeant that stood to the side.

_____

THE FIRST PALE LIGHT OF EARLY MORNING WASHED THE sides of the big barn that adjoined the Planters Hotel and the office of the stage line. Reuben and Elly were already busy rigging the two pack mules with the many supplies and other gear purchased the day before at Koch's emporium. The two horses they bought from the Applegate ranch, a blood sorrel mare with a blaze face and three stockings that stood fifteen two hands was Elly's, and a steel dust Gelding, black mane and tail at sixteen hands for Reuben, and both stood watching from the stalls, already saddled and ready for the day's journey.

The high-sided freight wagons were strung out beside the large corral behind the barn, and the teamsters were busy harnessing and hooking up their six-up mule teams. The stagecoach sat lonesome just back from the big door of the barn, sheltered in the dim light of the interior. The stage was not scheduled to leave until early morning but with the many changes in teams and tight schedule, it would easily overtake the freighters. Reuben planned for an early start wanting to be well on the way before the stage took to its route.

The creak and rattle of a buckboard entering the big barn alerted Reuben to the arrival of the gold chests. The wagon held the driver and three guards each armed with double barreled coach guns and attentive to all the activity around the barn. The driver called out to Reuben, "You the one what gets these chests! That so'jer boy said he'd be right along!"

"Set 'em down right there next to those other two!" ordered Reuben, pointing to the two chests that sat next to the door of the livery office.

The driver nodded to the three guards who hopped off the wagon, and with a quick look around, picked up the two small chests and stacked them beside the others. One of the guards asked, "You want us to stay and guard 'em?"

"No, we'll take 'em from here," answered Reuben, with a nod to the men. The three men hopped on the back of the wagon as the driver backed it out of the barn and drove it back into the street and past the bank. Reuben and Elly were alone in the barn for a short while before Whip's son, Captain Dodd, walked through the big doors with another officer at his side. He approached Reuben with a broad grin. "Reuben, this is Lieutenant Oscar Warner," as he nodded to his companion, "Lieutenant, this is Reuben Grundy and his wife, Elly."

The young officer stepped forward with his hand extended to Reuben. "Pleased to meet you," and with a glance to Elly, "Ma'am," and tipped his hat.

"Is everything ready?" asked the captain.

"It is, and if you'll give me a hand, we can put two of these in the coach," nodding to the chests and bending to grab one of the grips at the end of the top chest. They easily and quickly put one of the chests in the boot at the back of the coach and the other in the box beneath the driver's seat. They had no sooner stepped down from the stage than Henry Hatcher and one of his muleskinners pulled one of the freight wagons in front of the big doors of the barn and the big man hopped down, showing an unexpected agility for such a big man, and walked toward the men beside the coach. He looked at the two chests, glanced up at the captain and asked, "Those for me?"

The captain looked at Reuben and back to the muleskinner. "They are."

The big man grabbed the top chest, lifted it to his shoulder and returned to the freighter. Reuben was surprised to see the man straddle the tongue of the big wagon and slip open a hidden compartment and lift the chest into the hole, then return for the second chest. He grinned, "Didn't expect that, didja?" he chuckled as he looked at the captain with a cursory glance to Reuben.

"That's good. I don't reckon many would know of that hideout."

"Nope. I use it for special cargo. Most of my men don't know about it either. That freighter is my personal wagon." He placed the second chest in the compartment, slid the door closed and stepped back. "We're headin' out now!" he declared as he stepped on the hub of the wheel and up to the seat. With a nod to the captain and Reuben, he cracked his whip and started his freighter out, leading the others as they started out of town.

The freighters had just cleared the barn when Whip and Windy, two hostlers, and the four additional guards stepped through the big doors. Whip called out, "Wal, hello, Teddy! Didn't 'spect to see you here!"

"I guess you are getting ready to load up and leave?" replied the captain, grinning at his father.

"Yup. By the time we get hitched, pull 'er o'er to the office and load up the mail, cargo, and passengers, it'll be time to leave!"

The captain looked to his lieutenant. "Then you need to muster the troops. We'll be following close after the coach."

The lieutenant saluted, turned on his heel and left the barn at a quick step. The troops were bivouacked a short way from the edge of town and would be ready within the hour. The captain spoke with his father as the team of mules was getting hitched and neither man noticed as Reuben and Elly mounted up and left the barn from the back door by way of the corrals, leading their loaded packhorses and bound for the confluence of Cherry Creek and the South Platte River as the beginning point of their impending journey.

Although it was early morning when Reuben and Elly started from the Planters House, there were many men already rolling from their cabins and tents, anxious to try their luck at the sluice boxes that lined the banks of Cherry Creek and the South Platte. Many of these were Johnny-come-latelies that knew little or nothing of gold mining, and were scratching in diggings that had long been exhausted. Most of the gold mining activity had moved into the mountains to the boom-towns of Blackhawk and Mountain City where news still filtered down of rich strikes. The prospectors had followed the traces upstream of Clear Creek and worked hard at getting the rich ore from the stubborn mountains. As they passed the hopefuls bound to the west, many watched Reuben and Elly pay little attention to the miners and push on to the north, following the east bank of the South Platte River.

Longing for the fresh pine scented air, both Reuben and Elly were anxious to put the city and crowds of people behind them. It was good to feel the rocking gait of the horses, hear the creak of saddle leather, and even the dust of the trail was a pleasant change from their brief encounter with the bustling ways of the growing Denver City. Elly leaned back and took a deep breath of the country air, filling her lungs with the bittersweet juniper, the distant dusky smell of sage, and the sweet hint of cholla blossoms. Reuben grinned at his woman, reached down and stroked the neck of his steel dust, and looked back at Elly. "How ya likin' that sorrel?"

Elly turned to look at Reuben and mimicked his action of stroking the neck of her mount. "She's fine. She has an easy stride, nice and smooth, suits me!"

"You like her better than your Appaloosa?"

"I dunno. They're both fine animals, and I rode the Appy a bit more, you know, got used to her. But Red here is nice, smooth gait an' all."

"Well, we're gonna be on 'em several days. I figger on cuttin' northeast, away from the river and anglin' up toward Bijou Station, or thereabouts."

"How long you think it'll take us?"

"Couple days. I think we'll find us a place to hole up this afternoon, then take to the trail by moonlight. Not too anxious to run into some Arapaho or Cheyenne Dog Soldiers."

Elly chuckled. "After all the parties we been to with them, and you're still being anti-social?" Reuben shook his head, chuckling at his mischievous wife, knowing the last thing she wanted to do was the two-step with a raiding party of Indians.

He had no sooner spoken of angling to the northeast than they came to a bit of a confluence where a dry creek bed fed its runoff to the South Platte, but it was enough of a break in the terrain for Reuben to put the rising sun off his right shoulder and point the horses away from the river. It was dry land they were riding into, rolling hills covered with buffalo grass, blue gramma, sage and grease wood, rabbit brush and lots of cacti. The driftwood cactus, cholla, was showing its pink and yellow blossoms atop the spindly branches, the prickly pear patches were lifting big yellow and orange blossoms to the rising sun, and smaller bunches of hedgehog were displaying the brilliant red blossoms in a bunch. With the added clusters of Indian Paintbrush orange flowers, the rolling plains looked like the Creator had played hopscotch across the land, splashing colors at random to decorate an otherwise dreary land.

Reuben reined up atop a slight rise, leaned on the pommel of his saddle and said, "You know, God musta had a lot of fun paintin' this world, don'tcha think?"

Elly smiled broadly, let a little giggle escape. "You know, for such a big, rough looking and talking man, you sure see the wonders of His creation through gentle eyes. Maybe that's one of the many reasons I love you!"

"Look there," he added, pointing back along the trail they had followed, "looks like some wagons of 'go-backers' that Windy had talked about. Musta found the mountains and gold-minin' a little more difficult than they thought it would be when they left the east."

"But isn't this still Indian territory?" asked Elly, frowning at the slow-moving wagons that trailed behind the lumbering oxen.

"Yes, it is, well, sort of anyway." He waved his arm toward the east and north. "All this was part of the land that was said to belong to the Cheyenne and Arapaho under the 1851 Fort Laramie treaty, but the Fort Wise treaty that Little Raven spoke about, took most of this from them in exchange for $30,000 in annuities every year and peace with the whites, and relegated them to less land to the south just this side of the Arkansas River.

But Little Raven and most of the others didn't understand the treaty and did not willingly give up the best of their buffalo huntin' territory. And the government never paid their annuities and the gold-seekers kept comin'."

"Looks like a bunch of dry land that's not good for much," observed Elly.

"Buffalo like it, and the natives like the buffalo," resolved Reuben, nudging his steel dust to move out.

"What's that?" asked Elly, pointing to a thin spiral of smoke several miles away but in the direction they were heading.

Reuben stopped his grey, reached for his binoculars, and took a gander through the glasses. "Can't tell from here but looks to me to be more than a campfire, not big enough for a prairie fire, but I'm guessin' it's not good." With a glance back toward the two wagons, he nodded. "Let's get a move on and see what that is 'fore them greenhorns run into trouble."

The rolling hills of the plains can be very deceiving. At first glance, the land appears to stretch forever, tall grasses waving in the gentle breezes, and shows itself flat in the hazy distance. But the gently rolling terrain can hide an entire native village, a winding wagon train, a war party of raiding Dog soldiers and more as the land dips and rises with nothing to distinguish the swales and swells. The trail followed by Reuben and Elly had been well traveled over the past two years by the many gold-seekers and go-backers, with the Smoky Hill trail, the Overland Trail and the cutoff from the Overland covering the same land. They had covered the short distance from Denver City where the Smoky Hill trail and the cutoff had joined, but Reuben could see the smoke was coming from just beyond the convergence of the two trails.

As they topped a slight rise, Reuben reined up as he stared at the gruesome sight of the remains of burning wagons. Elly came alongside and he said, "Looks like three, maybe four wagons. Don't know if they were headin' back east or..." he let the thought hang as the breeze brought the stench of burning flesh over them. Reuben lifted his neckerchief to cover his mouth and nose, nudged the steel dust forward as he slipped the Henry from the scabbard beneath his right leg to lay it across the pommel. He jacked a round into the chamber and gently lowered the hammer. Elly copied her husband's actions, and he heard her jack a round into the chamber of her Henry and was pleased with her action.

As they neared the sight, there was no sign of life. The wagons had apparently made camp near a cluster of junipers in a slight niche of the hills near the green of a trickling stream that came from a spring back in the trees. It was a well-chosen site for a camp, but not a good one for defense in the event of an attack. Reuben was quick to read the sign and saw the tracks of many raiders, undoubtedly natives, that had swarmed the wagons and killed or captured everyone and ransacked the wagons before setting them on fire. All that remained were the steel rims of the wheels and parts of the wagons, a few charred boards, broken dishes, smashed pots and pans, and the bodies of at least five people, apparently all men.

Reuben rode a circuit of the wagons, ensuring there was no further danger, and returned to where Elly waited, then stepped down. He looked at her and said, "Reckon I better see 'bout buryin' these folks. Found a shovel yonder, so I'll dig a spot near the trees there'bouts," nodding to the shade that stretched from the junipers. "Might as well step down, stretch your legs. There's some grass near the water yonder; maybe the horses would like a bite or two."

Elly swung a leg over the rump of her sorrel and hopped to the ground. She grabbed up the reins of her sorrel and Reuben's steel dust, the leads of the mules and led them to the grass and water. While they buried their noses in the water, she loosened the girths and let them shake a little as they pushed one another about trying for the best of the grass. She looked about, frowning, then asked, "The natives don't usually like the mules, you think they just had horses?"

"Musta. The tracks don't show mules, so prob'ly."

Reuben used the remnant of a blanket to drag the desecrated and mutilated bodies to the grave. It would be a common grave and he was ready to start covering the bodies until Elly called, "Reuben, there's another." Her voice came from the trees, and he followed the sound of her voice, dragging the blanket behind. Elly stood over the body of a woman and held out her hand for the blanket. She lay it over the body and gently rolled the body onto the blanket, covering it as best she could. The woman had been viciously used and left bloody and mutilated. Tears filled Elly's eyes as she struggled with the task, but she wrapped the body as best she could, stood and nodded to Reuben.

He filled in the grave, carried several stones to cover the fresh soil and protect the bodies from scavengers, and stood, looking at the grave as Elly came to his side and pushed the Bible into his hand. He flipped it open to a familiar passage and began reading the 23rd Psalm aloud, *The Lord is my shepherd...*" and continued through the passage, Elly leaning against his shoulder and tears filling her eyes. He continued through the last verse, *"Surely goodness and mercy shall follow me all the days of my life: and,"* but as he came to the last phrase, they were startled when two tiny voices spoke the last words as Reuben read, *"I will dwell in the house of the Lord forever."* They turned to see two youngsters, a boy of about ten and a girl of about eight, holding hands, dirty tear-stained faces, looking lost and afraid, but standing and staring at the fresh grave and the two strangers before them.

"Our Momma taught us that verse," said the boy, wiping tears from his dirty face.

17 / ENCOUNTER

E lly dropped to one knee, holding her arms out wide and smiling at the two urchins, bidding them come into her embrace. The two looked at her, one another, and ran into the waiting arms, tears flowing freely. When Elly wrapped her arms around them and hugged them close, sobs came from all three as they squeezed one another. Elly glanced over at Reuben who dabbed at the corners of his eyes as he looked away from the heartrending scene and she mouthed the words, "Now what?"

Reuben stepped closer and said, "Follow me, there's a spot just over that shoulder we can make camp. There's a bit of grass and water and we'll just rest up and think things out."

Elly stood, taking each one of the children's hands in her own and spoke softly, "Let's go with Reuben and maybe we can find you something to eat. Would that be all right?"

The boy sniffed, nodding as he looked up at Elly and said, "I'm Micah and my sister's name is Mary." Reuben led the horses and mules and walked around the junipers to mount the slight shoulder that dropped them into another horseshoe shaped basin cradled in the low hillside. A small cluster of junipers with a couple gnarly cedar offered some shade and Reuben stripped the bedrolls from the cantles, tossed them in the shade and began stripping the gear from each of the animals. Elly had the youngsters help her roll out the bedrolls and then went to the parfleche for some smoked meat. She took a couple of bits of cloth, wet them down, and did a little face washing while they sat in the shade and worked on the strips of meat. Elly inquired, "Were you folks heading back east or going to the mountains?"

"Pa and the others had their fill of prospectin' and decided to go back to Missouri and get back to farmin'. They said raisin' crops paid better'n they were makin' with the sluice boxes," answered Micah, sounding very grown up for such a young man.

"Do you have other family back in Missouri?" asked Elly.

"Yes, ma'am. We have an Uncle and Aunt and their kids that had the farm next to ours. They were supposed to work the farm until they heard from Pa. Don't know what they'll do now."

Their conversation was interrupted by the cracking of whips and shouting of men as they pushed the yoke of oxen pulling the wagons. It was the group of travelers seen by Reuben and Elly from atop the ridge before they came to the burnt-out wagons. Reuben walked back to the crest of the shoulder that separated them from the site of the attack. The people of the wagons had come near, pulled up and were walking toward the remains when they saw Reuben standing to the side. One of the men called out, "Ho there! You part of these wagons?"

motioning to the remains that still emitted a puff of smoke with the passing breeze.

Reuben walked to meet the travelers, shaking his head and as he neared, he answered, "Nope! Came upon 'em a short while ago. Buried the bodies yonder," motioning to the new grave site with his chin and looked back at the gathering men that were moving around for a better look at the remains. Reuben noted they were a rough looking group, probably unsuccessful prospectors that had soured on everything and everyone. He judged them to be the type that blamed everyone but themselves for their failures. And his initial opinion was confirmed when the bigger of the men said, "Thought we'd check an' see if there was anythin' worth salvagin'." No thought or concern about the people, just about anything they could claim for themselves.

"Nope, everythin's been destroyed or taken by the raiders," answered Reuben, looking at the men. There were six of them, all a little scruffy looking, tattered clothing, dirty and unkempt, and he did not like the way several of them kept glancing his way as if they were waiting for something to happen. He was a little surprised to see their type driving oxen and wagons, and wondered where they managed to get enough money to stake themselves to the gear for their journey. Reuben turned away a mite and asked, "You men headin' back east?"

"Ummhmm," answered the big man as he nodded to the others to look over the remains of the other wagons with nothing more than a glance to Reuben.

Reuben grinned to himself, holding the side of his jacket closed to obscure his holstered pistol, but immediately felt a little uncomfortable being outnumbered by such a bunch and began to work his way a few steps up the shoulder of the hillside away from them. He saw the group trying to position themselves around him without looking at him as he turned away and reached inside his jacket to grasp the butt of the Remington pistol. When he looked back at the men, the big man grinned and said, "We'll just take whatever you got to make up for these wagons," and chuckled as he motioned to the men to move in on him.

Reuben backstepped as he drew the pistol, aiming it directly at the head of the big man, "You can try!" he declared.

His action stopped the others, but one of the men had also started to draw his pistol, but the bark of a Henry rifle from behind a clump of sage at the crest of the shoulder ridge stopped his movement and stopped the others where they stood. Wide-eyed they looked at the sagebrush but saw only the thin wisp of smoke curling upwards from the barrel but the unmistakable clatter of jacking a shell into the chamber made the men look at one another and at the big man who was staring down the barrel of Reuben's Remington.

With a calm, quiet voice, Reuben said, "I suggest you fellas get back to your wagons and get a move on down the trail. You have a long ways to go and between here and nightfall, you just might run into some of our friends, either the Arapaho or the Cheyenne Dog Soldiers, and you might want to save yourselves for fightin' them."

The group of men looked to one another and one of the whiskery faced men looked at his leader, "Bull! I thought you said there weren't no Injuns if we come thisaway!"

The big man growled, "He don't know nuthin'! That

so'jer boy tol' me they done whipped them Injuns, put 'em on a reservation down south!"

Reuben grinned, chuckling. "Then why don't you just go back to your wagons and keep on goin'?" waving his pistol as he spoke. He had noticed one of the men to his left was trying to work his way up the slope to get closer to Reuben, and the Henry barked again, the bullet striking a rock beside the man's foot and ricocheting with a whine just past the man's head, making him dive to the ground.

"Next time, there won't be a warnin' shot," he declared. "And it'll be a toss-up which one of us gets to score the hit!" He waved his pistol again, raised his voice and commanded, "NOW GIT!!" prompting all the men to turn and quickly make their way back to the wagons, their grumbling and fussing heard all the way. Once they were far enough away to pose no threat, Reuben holstered his pistol and walked up the slope, grinning as Elly stood from behind the sage, Henry in hand and smiling broadly. "The kids?"

She nodded toward the camp where the youngsters were sitting in the shade, holding on to one another and watching as Reuben and Elly walked back. The sounds of the wagons told they were on the move and Reuben stepped away from the camp, closer to the trail, to watch and be certain all the men were with the wagons, and none had hung back for some nefarious purpose. It was easy to count the men with one in the seat of each wagon and one on either side of the yoke of oxen, the six were accounted for and several gave a snarling glance toward Reuben as he watched them leave.

He walked back to the camp, grabbed a handful of smoked meat from the open parfleche and sat down in the shade by the others. Micah said, "I was worried they were some of those that attacked us."

Reuben frowned, looked at the boy. "These were all white men, Micah. Wasn't it Indians that attacked your wagons?"

"That's what we thought at first, but after Pa hid us in the trees, we could see and there were some white men with the Indians."

"Are you sure?"

"Yessir. There were three of 'em. Lots more Indians, but three men like you."

Reuben looked at Elly and back at Micah. The boy added, "One of the men was tellin' the others what to do and they took our Mama to the trees. She screamed a lot."

Reuben looked at Elly. "That means renegades; that's worse. A raidin' party of Arapaho or Cheyenne, but renegades have no compunction about anythin'!" He looked around, thinking, stood, and walked about the camp, then stopped, looking at Elly. "I'll gather up some firewood, enough for a bit of a fire for supper. Then I'm gonna climb this little knoll, take a good look-see with my glasses. We'll wait till full dark then move out and travel by moonlight. It'll be safer, especially with the young'uns."

With his Sharps in hand, the telescope mounted, and the binoculars dangling around his neck, Reuben mounted the slight knoll and took a seat beside a scraggly piñon. With his knees drawn up, to use for his elbow rest, he began a scan of the flats in all directions. Although he considered it important to always be aware of their surroundings, this time was as much for him to do some thinking as it was to scout the terrain.

Although he knew this route had an increased danger

of detection by both the Arapaho and the Cheyenne, he had chosen this way to keep anyone that had been watching their movements and those of the freighters and stagecoach, from thinking they were in anyway connected with the gold shipment. Or just the opposite, to confuse the planning of anyone bound to attack the gold shipment, to at least make them account for Reuben and Elly and their involvement if any. Either way, he believed they had been watched and even followed a little way as they left Denver City, but he did not think anyone continued to follow them.

Now, everything had become much more complicated with a band of renegades on the prowl, using the fear of Indian attack to mask their assaults and destruction, and with the youngsters in their hands and needing to be protected. He was already calculating ways to get the children safely back to their family in Missouri, but until they could reach the stage stations, they were obligated to protect them. And the dangers like the one they just encountered was another factor he had not considered.

He shook his head as he cleared his mind to scan the terrain. The clear day, not a cloud in the sky, gave him a visibility of several miles in every direction and the only thing he spotted was the dwindling dust of the two wagons, a few deer at the edge of a trickle of a stream making its way north to the South Platte, and a band of antelope grazing in the distance, unalarmed and unconcerned. He started to lower his glasses when movement caught his eye and he focused on a distant draw, probably four or more miles to the northeast, near the trail. Several horses came from the draw, all ridden by natives, after the two wagons passed. It was evident by their action they had seen the wagons, and the band, he counted sixteen, appeared to be a hunting party, but it was difficult to tell from this distance. He continued to watch as they rode to the north, apparently bound for the South Platte river-flats, where the game would be plentiful. He continued to watch until they were swallowed by a deep draw and were too far away when they emerged, still heading north.

Reuben slowly stood, looking around to be certain he did not give himself away, and moved away from the crest, walking down the slope to return to the now quiet camp. As he came close, he saw Micah on his bedroll, lying on his side, his knees drawn up, and sound asleep. Mary was wrapped in Elly's arms and the two were smiling in their sleep, probably the safest the little girl had felt since the early morning attack on the wagons. Reuben smiled, grabbed a handful of smoked meat, and returned to his promontory beside the piñon, to keep watch and wait for the darkness.

T he moon stood high over the eastern horizon that was marked by the black silhouette that appeared more as a dividing line between darkness and the pale blue light of the waxing moon. Scattered clouds dimpled the night sky, masking the shimmering jewels of the night. The cool of the evening made each of the travelers hunker into the collars of their jackets and the two youngsters to huddle up to their rescuers. Mary sat behind the pommel, sharing the seat of the saddle with Elly while Micah sat atop the bedroll behind Reuben, his hands tucked into the pockets of Reuben's jacket. The loaded pack mules took an easy stride behind the horses, and the night sounds masked the creak of saddle leather.

A coyote sky-lined himself as he lifted his nose to the stars and began his mournful song in hopes of finding his companion, but went unanswered. Crickets rattled their chorus across the flats through the sage, and the muted flapping of wings warned of the silent hunter of the night as he swooped down to catch an after-curfew prairie dog for his supper. They rode silently, the youngsters leaning against their protectors and dozing as they rocked with the gait of the horses.

It had been most of two hours when Reuben gave a silent signal and nudged his mount into the low swale of a dry gulch, taking to the grey barked cottonwoods and the many saplings for cover. He reined up, stepped down with his Henry in hand, and handed the reins of his steel dust to Micah and whispered to Elly, "I smelled dust. Somethin's movin' out there; might be nothin' but a couple buffalo, but I want to make sure." Elly nodded and twisted around to pull Mary close as she pushed her sorrel beside the steel dust and Micah. She watched as Reuben silently climbed the sandy bank of the draw and disappeared behind the treetops.

The moon was high overhead and the shadows of the night had grown short as Reuben went to one knee, the trees behind him to mask his image in the dim moonlight. Then he saw them, the returning band of natives, pushing a small herd of horses probably taken from some ranch near the South Platte River and leading a couple of horses with bodies draped over their backs. They had been in a battle and taken their licks as well as capturing the horses. Reuben frowned, squinting to try to see better, wondering if they had any captives but he could not see any; all appeared to be warriors. As he watched, the band moved across the trail and into the rolling hills to the south, yet he continued to look for any warriors that followed, mindful of their backtrail. Satisfied they were well into the southern hills, he walked back to the others and mounted up to continue their journey.

They stopped shortly after midnight to give the horses a breather and let the youngsters stretch their legs and have a bite to eat but were soon back on the trail.

They passed a couple camps of wagons and judging from their tracks, most were returning to the east. The tracks of the wagon wheels covering the tracks of the mules pulling them was the giveaway as to the direction they were traveling. Reuben chuckled to himself at the nature of man always wanting riches but also wanting it in some easy way. He had never been one that was swayed by the riches of others or even the things that great wealth could provide. A man of simple tastes that was more interested in the challenges of life and the variety of God's creation, he preferred to make his own way than to be hindered by the problems of wealth.

It was coming on morning as the thin line of grey parted the horizon from the night sky, and the stars began snuffing out their lanterns when Reuben began watching for a camp for the weary travelers. Spotting a low bluff with a stretch of rimrock overhanging a thicket of junipers, he nudged the steel dust to the site. Satisfied with his choice, he swung his leg over the gelding's neck, slid to the ground and reached up to help Micah down. He gave Elly a hand with a sleeping Mary, and once he put her down with her head in Micah's lap, he helped Elly to the ground. He spoke softly to her, "After I strip the animals, I'll get us some firewood and we can have a small fire for some coffee and bacon, maybe some flapjacks for the little ones."

Elly giggled as she poked Reuben in the belly. "The little ones, my eye!"

Reuben chuckled. "Then I'm goin' up top here to look around." He had an armload of dry firewood and dropped it by the circle of rocks Elly had arranged, then turned away and was stopped when he heard gunfire. He frowned, grabbed up his Sharps and the binoculars and quickly mounted the bluff. The gunfire was sporadic and from a short distance away, by the sound of it he guessed it to be maybe a mile or two, prompting him to drop to one knee and lift the glasses to search the hills to the northeast. Whatever was happening, was in the bottom of a swale and hidden from sight, but he knew it was not good. He searched the flats for any movement, but there was none. Still the sounds of battle came unbidden. He quickly returned to camp and began re-saddling the steel dust. Elly came to his side. "What is it?"

"I dunno. Couldn't see. I'm guessin' it's the same renegades that hit their folks," nodding to the little ones. "I've gotta go see if I can help. You know what to do if I don't come back; stay to the northeast, travel at night, and you should come to the Overland trail and the stage stations."

"You just come back to me!"

They looked at one another, embraced, and Reuben swung aboard his mount. He was armed well with the Henry in one scabbard, the Sharps in the other, and he had strapped the Spencer behind the cantle of the saddle. The saddle bags were heavy with ammunition. As they looked at one another, they both knew this would be the first time they could not back up one another; the youngsters required the protection of Elly and she felt helpless as she watched Reuben kick his mount to a canter as he headed into the rising sun to do what he seemed to always do; help someone else.

The rising sun was blazing above the eastern horizon, long lances of bright orange tinged with red shot into the heavens while the underbellies of scattered clouds were pregnant with color. At any other time, Reuben would have reined up and sat in wonder at the palette of color used by the Creator on such an ordinary day, but the rattle of gunfire kept his attention as he used the contours of the land to obscure his approach. He was close enough to hear the cacophony of battle made memorable by the screams of war cries, the panicked neighs of wounded and dying horses, the shouts of combatants and the staccato rattle of rifle fire. The smell of gunpowder mixed with the dust of the attackers and the smoke of cookfires stung his senses.

As he came to a cluster of alders and willows in the bottom of a draw, swung down, Spencer in hand. Tethering the grey, he began working his way closer to the fight, crawling on all fours and using the tall grasses, sage, and greasewood for cover. A slight knoll with a twisted cedar atop offered a bit of a promontory and he made his way to the scraggly tree.

Just below, no more than seventy yards distant, the two wagons of the men that had accosted him the day before, were side by side. All the oxen were sprawled about, dead or dying, the horses that had been tethered behind the wagons were nowhere to be seen, and he spotted at least two bodies of the men near the wagons. Gun smoke lay low like a wispy grey cloud, obscuring the others from Reuben's view, but he could see the attackers hunkered down behind a couple of the dead oxen, clusters of sage and rocks. Their assault seemingly undiminished, but Reuben spotted at least three dead attackers, one obviously a white man. *These are the renegades!* whispered Reuben, shaking his head as he brought his Spencer up. He paused as he considered what he was about to do, it might be better just to let them kill each other off, for neither bunch was what anyone would call 'good people'. If he jumped in on the side of the men with the wagons, they would probably just rob some other 'go-backers' as they attempted to rob him. But if he let the renegades wipe them out, they would keep attacking other travelers and kill innocent families like they did before.

He had a good field of fire, situated as he was above and to the side of the battle. All the attackers, and he had picked out at least eight of them, were exposed to his position. But he waited, wanting to be certain of the position of all the attackers before he gave away his position. He looked about to choose his second and third firing position, knowing as soon as he fired the first round or two, he must move before they could mark his spot and return fire. He picked his shots, choosing the two white men on the far side first, then others of the renegade natives, for as soon as he fired the first shot, they would know they were exposed and move.

He knew the first shot would be a surprise, most not recognizing there was another shooter, and he carefully drew his bead on the man behind the tall sage at the far side of the swale. The man was on one knee, lining up his own shot at the wagons, when Reuben dropped the hammer. The big Spencer roared, bucked, and spat smoke and lead, sending the .52 caliber slug on its way to bury itself under the arm of the outlaw, plowing through his torso and out the other side, taking the man's life with it.

Reuben dropped the lever, jacked another cartridge into the chamber and eared back the big hammer as he swung his sights to the second man who had looked at his partner on his left. Before he could react, another big slug slammed into the side of his head, blowing a hole the size of a fist on the far side, knocking him to the ground to lie in a puddle of his own blood.

Reuben crabbed back from the tree, just below the rise of the hill and quickly moved to his left to a big clump of greasewood for his second position, jacking another cartridge into the chamber and earing back the hammer as he moved. He was quickly in position, found his next target and saw the renegades showing confusion as they looked to the crest of the low bluff where the tangled cedar stood. The Spencer roared again, taking the third man just behind the shoulder, shattering his clavicle and driving through his chest taking the bear claw necklace with it as it blasted out the other side. The renegade was dead before he knew he had been hit and fell face first into the sage.

Reuben moved again, taking his third position behind some rocks and quickly found his next target. The firing from the wagons increased, probably realizing they had an ally, and the renegades were fidgety, realizing they no longer had the advantage and searching for a way back to their horses. But the Spencer roared again, and another renegade screamed as he stood, back arching and chest blossoming red before he fell, never to rise again. The rest of the renegades jumped and ran for their horses and Reuben let them go, but several of those at the wagons sent another volley that dropped another renegade, wounded another that stumbled, fell, and rose again to get to his horse. Reuben was satisfied, crawled back away from the rocks, and quickly returned to his own horse. He had no desire to talk to the men of the wagons, only wanting to return to Elly and the youngsters to ensure they were safe.

E agle's Station was nothing more than a quick stop for the stages. With only a house, barn, and corral, they seldom had more than a change of teams for the stages and never provided a meal stop. The first station to the east of the Latham, and last station on the west bound line before Latham, the hostlers made a quick switch of the teams and sent the stages on their way. So it was a surprise to the men at the station when, just at the break of day, three men stormed through the door, guns blazing to kill everyone at the station. The men were caught in their bunks and had no chance to defend themselves and when Crocket looked at Stink who was grinning and laughing at the dead men sprawled half off their bunks, blood pooling on the dirt floor beside them, Crocket just shook his head and ordered Stink and Baldy, "Come on! Let's get outta here! We gotta set the ambush with Faraday!" With a last glance around, Crocket followed the two men outside to mount up and head to their rendezvous with the Rebs. Before leaving, they opened the gate to the big corral and spooked all the horses and mules out of the corral and into the flats beyond the trail.

The Overland Trail road was always within sight of the South Platte, but with the meandering river, the trail was often closer to the riverbank and the few trees, cottonwood, alders and willows. It was at one of these bends in the southeast bound river that Confederate Captain George Madison, otherwise known as Captain Faraday, when he was arrayed in blue, chose to set the ambush and it was here that he met up with Crocket and his outlaws. When Crocket rode into the trees he nodded to the captain, the only man in full uniform proudly displaying his butternut and grey with the trimming all in the butternut, and swung down, handing the reins to his mount to Stink and motioning for him and Baldy to tether the mounts further in the trees and return. Crocket stepped to the side of the captain, "Captain," he said as he snapped a salute which the captain returned, "the station at Eagle's Nest is secured, sir."

"Good, good. The stage will be coming along shortly, the horses will be tired and the troops out front will be easy targets. Sergeant, I want you and your men to take three others out there, on the other side of the trail where the sage is tall, station them under cover and wait for our signal. I'll start things with my shot. My men and I will be along the bank here and between here and the trail using the sage and rocks," motioning with a head nod toward the cover indicated. "The driver and shotgunner are civilians, so don't make them targets unless the shotgunner joins the fight. But our scouts said there are additional guards, prob'ly troopers in civies, and they are to be taken out." He paused, judging the sergeant's response, and continued, "Lieutenant Washington is with the rest of the men back up the trail. They will be the decoy to stop the other troops that are following. Once we have the gold, we'll immediately break off and leave the area."

"What about the stage and passengers?" asked Sergeant Crocket.

"Leave 'em be," and with a nod to the northwest along the trail, they saw the rising dust cloud that told of the approaching stage.

"Yessir," replied the sergeant as he turned away to select those that would be with his men in the ambush and quickly led them across the trail to find their cover.

THE FIRST VOLLEY FROM THE HIDDEN GUERRILLA BAND OF confederates was a blistering and deadly hail of lead. The six troopers that lined out in front of the stage took the barrage and most fell from their horses. The captain took two slugs that unseated him and dropped him in the dirt, four troopers suffered fatal wounds and two were taken from the fight. One stayed aboard his horse and charged past the attackers to find refuge in the trees. The four troopers acting as guards were all atop the stage and were not the initial targets, but the surprise attack caught them unprepared, and they scrambled for any position or cover among the gear, only two returned fire.

Whiskers and Levi had replaced Whip and Windy as driver and guard at Latham and neither took lead, but Whiskers was quick to let loose his ten-gauge coach gun and was rewarded with the obliterated face of one of the attackers. Whiskers was quick to lay out the whip to kick the six-up of horses into a gallop and the dust cloud obscured the firing of the attackers, but the guards atop the stage took their toll with two of the attackers downed.

"AFTER 'EM!" shouted the confederate captain as he snatched up the reins of his own mount and swung aboard as the horse gave chase. Five men were quick to follow the captain, and the dust churned around them. Yet in less than a mile, the rebels had overtaken the stage, killing two of the guards up top and losing one of their own before Whiskers reined in the team. Levi had taken a slug in his side and was bent over, his shotgun across his lap.

Behind them in the distance, the sounds of battle carried on the wind and the captain glanced to Sergeant Crocket, grinning as the passengers were rousted out of the stage to stand beside the road, hands held high. With a nod to the sergeant, he commanded, "Get the strongboxes! There's two of 'em!" He looked at the driver and shotgunner. "Keep your hands high till we're gone, and you'll live to see the sunset!" chuckling as he spoke. The body of one of the guards lay in blood atop the stage, the other had fallen off in the chase. The remaining two guards were grumbling but held their hands high, watching the band of rebels retrieve the chest from the driver's box while others ransacked the boot for the second box. They threw luggage and mail sacks aside, snatched up the box and shouted, "We got it!"

"Corporal Whittaker! Go back and give the other troops the signal to break off the attack and come after us!" shouted the captain to a tousle-headed young man that wore a butternut and grey uniform jacket and cap that showed two stripes on the arm. There were a few others among the troops that had uniforms or portions of uniforms, but it was not unusual for any troop to be arrayed in a hodge-podge of homemade uniforms or any combination they could find.

"Yessir!" shouted the young non-comm as he swung back aboard his mount and took off at a gallop, anxious to please his commanding officer. He carried a guidon of red, white and blue with a white star, to give the signal and when he neared the battle, he searched for high ground and rode his mount to the top of a low bluff and began to furiously wave the guidon back and forth. The scene that lay below overwhelmed him as he saw a field and roadway littered with bodies and blood. Wounded men lay crying for help, a low wispy cloud of gun smoke floated like a blanket of the feathery seeds of a milkweed. The rifle fire began to diminish as the guerrillas broke cover and went to their horses. When the Union forces saw the attackers leaving, they stopped their firing except for a few that took a parting shot. Within a few moments, the remains of the attacking band were riding hard into the flats, following the corporal with the guidon.

WHEN THE ATTACKERS DISAPPEARED OVER THE LOW RISE to the south, Whiskers turned to Levi. "Let me look at that!" he growled as he pushed Levi's hand aside to look at the wound. "Looks like it went through, but it's bleeding purty good." He reached between his feet to a small pouch he kept in the boot and extracted some bandages and ointment. He rubbed two bandages with the dark thick goo and put one each on the front and back of the wound and struggled to wrap a wide band of cloth around his middle to hold them in place. Levi winced as the driver did his work, then asked, "What is that stuff anyhow?"

"Axle grease!" answered Whiskers, grinning at his friend. "If it don't fix ya' at least you won't squeak when you move!"

"I don't squeak now!"

"No, you just whine a lot!"

Whiskers turned his attention to the passengers and instructed them to pick up the luggage and bags and return them to the boot so they could get back on the trail. The passengers, grumbling and moaning, did as they were bidden, knowing most of the luggage was their own. While they were busy, Whiskers checked with the remaining guards, had them cover up the body of the dead man and promised to have someone pick up the body of their friend on the return trip. One of the men asked, "What about the others that took that first blast?"

"Reckon your fellow troopers that were behind us will hafta tend to them. I've got a schedule to keep," and within a few moments, Whiskers cracked his whip and had them back on the move.

LIEUTENANT WARNER WATCHED THE BAND OF confederate guerrillas disappear over the low rise and took a deep breath of relief, shaking his head and looking at his trembling hands. It had been a fearful fight and he had lost many men, but they had quickly found cover in a rocky draw and made a fight of it, defending themselves honorably. He stood and looked around at the men who sat back against the side draw, relieved the fight was over and they were still alive. He gave them a few moments as he walked among them, surveying the wounded, and counting the dead. There were three wounded, and he thought each one would survive their wounds. Nine were dead, out of twenty troopers. It was a terrible toll, but they had also dealt the enemy a hard hand. "Whitcomb! Help those wounded men, bind 'em up, do what'chu can."

He turned back to the others and spoke to them, "Alright men, the sooner we get after it, the sooner we're done. We've got to bury these men. Lewis, you get the personal belongings, put 'em in a bag and keep 'em till we get back. Everyone else, fetch your spades and go to work!" Once the men were busy at their tasks, the lieutenant walked among the bodies of the confederates and counted twelve, which did not include any wounded that were able to ride away. "Corporal MacIntosh! Get two men to help you and drag these bodies into that ravine yonder and cave the bank over the dead. Don't want 'em stinkin' up the countryside!" It was the right thing to do, but there was something about treating those that had so treacherously dealt death to their fellow soldiers that grated, but decency bid him do right.

They were on the trail by midday, hoping to catch up to the coach at the next station but they found the scene of the first ambush and reined up beside the dead. The lieutenant stepped down, heard something in the brush and pushed through the willows to find the wounded captain and two wounded troopers. "Captain, you hit bad?" he asked as he moved closer.

"Took a couple, my side," he groaned as he tried to move, "and my shoulder. If you can patch me up, I can prob'ly make it." He exhaled heavily, sucking in a big breath to stay the pain. The lieutenant hurried to his bag and retrieved some bandages and went to work. The captain struggled but was well tended by the lieutenant. He nodded his appreciation and suggested, "Let's have a meal and some coffee 'fore we do anything, whatsay?"

The lieutenant grinned and nodded. "Sounds good to me."

The captain looked at his junior officer and asked, "What's the tally?"

"Counting those here, thirteen dead, six wounded, counting you."

The captain shook his head, and the lieutenant continued, "We were outnumbered two to one, but we killed a dozen of them and there were three dead here. No tellin' how many wounded." Five more graves had to be dug and the weary men alternated the duty until all the dead were underground.

As is always the way with uniformed warriors, a bit of a rest and some food for their bellies does wonders for their strength and morale. Once the coffee was gone and the rest had rallied, they were feeling somewhat better and ready to return to Latham. "What about the stage?" asked the lieutenant.

"They're on their own now. This was as far as we were supposed to go anyway. But if they survived, the next station will tend to them, and if not, the next stage coming through will have to do it. We're in no shape for another fight, so, let's go home, or at least to Latham!"

"Suits me!" answered the lieutenant.

R euben came suddenly awake as Elly was shaking his shoulder. He frowned as she whispered, "There's dust, a lot of it, to the northwest. Looks like a big bunch of riders. I can't tell if they're Indians or..." She shrugged to show her confusion. She had been standing watch to give Reuben a time of rest, and brought the alarm as needed.

Reuben rolled from his blankets, took the offered binoculars, and snatched up his Sharps to climb the rise of the butte with the rimrock that overshadowed their campsite. Elly followed close behind and once atop the butte, they hunkered down behind a rock outcropping and Reuben lifted the glasses. Elly pointed. "There, to the northwest," as she settled on a rock beside her man.

Reuben steadied the binoculars, his elbows on the rock before him, and focused them in on the distant dust cloud. The dust alone showed several riders, but as he focused, he saw the riders were not natives, but white men with an odd assortment of grey and butternut uniforms. He frowned as he said, "Confederates?" He shook his head and adjusted his position for a better look, refocusing the field glasses. "Hmmm, I'm bettin' those are the ones that Faraday, or whatever his name is, was leadin' to get the gold. But if they're goin' south, they either already hit the stage, or they were turned back."

"How far away are they?" asked Elly, looking over Reuben's shoulder.

"Oh, that's at least three, maybe four miles. The direction they're goin' they won't come near here." He moved the glasses about, looking for possible routes or camps for the outfit. He spotted a cluster of trees, most dead and grey, but a few showing green, that appeared as an oasis in the vast stretch of bunch grass and sage. He moved the glasses back to the Confederates and nodding, dropped the glasses to look at Elly. "I think they're headed to that patch of trees to the south of them, probably gonna take a midday break to rest the horses. If they hit the stage, that'll be where they break open the strong boxes."

Elly let a slow grin split her face as she chuckled. "I'd like to be close enough to see their expressions when they open 'em!"

Reuben chuckled, turned around to look the way they were headed. Their plan was to rest up here and move out after dark, but with the intruders to their domain, plans might have to change, and he wanted to be certain of their route. He calculated it to be about a full day or night's ride to reach the Overland trail and a stage stop, hopefully the Bijou Creek station, and he preferred to sit tight and wait till dark. As he scanned the trail he saw little cover, mostly tall bunch grass, sage, a bit of gramma, and not much else until they reached a low swale or low gulch. It was easy traveling, but dangerous. He was thinking about the youngsters that were sleeping in the shade below their promontory as

well as their own safety. With the remnant of the renegades somewhere ahead of them, maybe even the
survivors of the two wagons, and any number of hunting
or raiding parties of the Cheyenne and Arapaho, and
now the confederates behind them, it was getting a little
uncomfortable.

"If we have to move out before dark, we'll stick to the
low land between the hills, stay away from the trail, and
hope for the best. You go down with the young'uns, I'll
stay here and watch that bunch," nodding toward the
band of rebels.

Elly leaned over and gave him a quick kiss, hunkered
down to keep from sky-lining herself and started down
the slope to the camp. Reuben lifted his glasses to watch
the boys in grey and hope they were stopping at the oasis
by the trees. The band traversed the couple miles in
short order and as Reuben guessed, they went to the
trees. He shook his head and grinned as he pictured what
was about to happen.

———————

Captain Madison called out, "Sergeant Hennesey,
Sergeant Crocket, make sure the men tend to their
horses before themselves. Have a couple men get a small
fire going and put on some coffee then gather what
rations we have and assign some men to sort it out.
Sergeant Hennesey, bring those two chests over there by
that log, and we'll take a look at this gold that cost us so
many men!"

"Yessir," answered the two men in unison, saluting
and turning on their heel to do the captain's bidding.
The captain walked the short distance to the big grey log
and dropped down to the ground beside it, leaning back

and stretching out as he removed his hat from his sweating head. He wiped his forehead with his sleeve, sat the hat on the log and leaned back to relax more than he had in a long time. It always felt good to come from any skirmish successfully, even though they lost some good men, they had accomplished their mission.

He closed his eyes as he leaned back his head, finding comfort in this difficult place, until Sergeant Hennesey said, "Here's one of 'em, I'll fetch the other'n," and walked away, leaving the captain to enjoy his solitude. Within a few moments, the captain was roused by the sound of a heavy chest dropped to the ground and the exhale of an exerted sergeant. He opened his eyes to look at the two identical strongboxes, the lids secured by Polhem padlocks, a heavy cast iron padlock. The captain lifted the heavy lock, recognizing the type and realizing it would not be easily broken, but he was determined. "Sergeant, get a couple spades, put one under the lock and use the other like a pick to try to break it."

The sergeant did as ordered, and once the stationary spade was in place, began driving the other spade down with all the force he could muster, only to have it clang like an out-of-tune bell each time it was struck, but no damage was done. After several tries, he paused, looked at the captain. "This ain't doin' no good, Captain!"

"Try again, Sergeant, you can do it!"

Again, the sergeant whacked away at the lock, but the sturdy cast iron device held, refusing to give way. The sergeant, winded, bent over, hands on knees and looked up at the captain shaking his head. The captain ordered, "Get that big redhead, you know, the big guy that's 'bout the size of a draft horse; get him, let him give it a try."

The sergeant nodded, stood and turned to walk toward the men that were busy fixing something to eat, and hollered, "O'Reilly! Get over here!" A big man, standing well over six feet and weighing in at about two hundred fifty pounds, maybe more, stood and seemed to block out the sunlight, to answer, "Aye, Sergeant Major, an' how can I be of help?" His Irish brogue sometimes made it difficult to understand the man and often confused the sergeant major whether the man was answering or mocking him, but he was too big to question. The sergeant said, "The captain wants you to bust a lock," handing him the extra spade and motioning to the strongboxes.

"Aye, Sergeant, an' I'll be givin' it a go!" as he grasped the spade that looked more like a spoon in his hands and walked to the strongboxes. He looked at the captain, down at the boxes, and grasping the spade with both hands, he stretched high with the spade above his head and drove the steel blade down like he was driving a spear into the ground. The blade struck the lock, the box bounced, and the handle of the spade split and splintered like a piece of kindling. O'Reilly looked at the spade, then at the lock. "B'gosh and B'gorrah, I'ma thinkin' we'll hafta try somethin' else, Captain."

"Any ideas?"

The big man frowned, looking at the lock, and answered, "The only thing hard enough would be a rifle barrel, or perhaps a bullet."

The captain looked from the big man to the sergeant major, nodded. "Sergeant, try shooting the cussed thing. But take it over yonder first, I don't want to be hit by a ricochet!"

The sergeant looked at O'Reilly. "You heard him, carry 'em over yonder," motioning to the edge of the trees where there was nothing but deep grass. The big man did as ordered, dropped both boxes near one another and stepped back as the sergeant pulled his sidearm, a Colt Army 1860 taken from the body of a Union officer, and cocked the hammer. He aimed at the lock and squeezed off his shot. The pistol roared and bucked, a grey cloud of smoke lancing from the barrel to obscure the lock, and the sergeant stepped close to drop to one knee to examine the lock. He shook his head, stood, and took aim again. After three shots, the lock finally broke, and he removed the pieces from the hasp and was about to open the lid of the strongbox when the captain spoke from behind him, "I'll do that."

The sergeant moved aside to let the officer drop to one knee beside the box and grab the hasp to lift the lid. Expecting to see gleaming gold bars, the captain was surprised at the contents of the box. There were heavy bars, but they were dark grey. He lifted one, grabbed his belt knife and scratched the surface to reveal what he had expected. "Lead! These aren't gold! They're lead!" He stood, threw the one bar back into the box and turned to the sergeant. "Open that box!" he demanded, pointing to the other box.

The sergeant major did as bidden and was successful in breaking the second lock with two well placed shots, and before the smoke cleared, the captain was lifting the second lid to find just what he expected, more lead bars. He dropped the lid, kicked at the box, turned, and stomped back to the log, mumbling, and fussing with every step, kicking at every stick and rock in his way. The sergeant had never seen the captain have such a fit and he chuckled at the behavior of the man that was supposed to be a leader of men. He followed the captain and when the man sat on the log, shaking his head, the sergeant asked, "Now what?"

The captain was recalcitrant for a while before

answering, "That gold has to be somewhere; that banker, Dinwoodie, was adamant about the shipment going out and our scout saw the guards take those strongboxes to the barn to load 'em on the stage."

"But did he see them loaded?" asked the sergeant.

"No, but..." started the captain, then paused. "Get Corporal MacIntosh over here!" The sergeant jumped to go fetch the corporal and quickly returned with the tow-headed young man who stood at attention and saluted the captain. The captain returned the salute and asked, "You were the scout that watched the loading of the stage, now tell me what you saw."

"Well, sir, as you ordered, I was across the street from the barn and watched as the wagon and guards came from the bank with those strongboxes. They drove the wagon into the barn, but I could still see 'em, and they unloaded the boxes, stacked 'em on some other boxes and left. When they did, they closed the barn door, but it was still open a little and I stayed to watch. Then a freighter pulled up outside and a big man stepped down and went in the barn. 'Bout that time a couple Union boys went in and I ducked back in the saloon 'fore they come out. I didn't want 'em seein' me watchin' 'em."

"So you did not see them load the strongboxes on the stage?"

"No, sir, I couldn't see what they were doin' inside the barn."

"Did the freighter leave before the stage?"

"Yessir, the big man checked the trace lines and such before he climbed back atop, then they pulled out with the other freighters."

"That was before the stage?"

"Yessir."

The captain thought about it a moment, looked back

up at the corporal and asked, "When the teamster checked the trace lines, could he have loaded something on the wagon?"

"Uh, I dunno, sir. He was on the other side of the team, and I couldn't see him all that well. But I reckon he could have, but it couldn'tna been too big cuz he didn't put anythin' in the wagon box."

The captain let a slow grin split his face as he stood, shaking his head, and looking at the sergeant. "Get the men ready to move out! We're goin' back to the stage road. Those freighters move a lot slower than the stage and I think they've got the gold! We'll hit them and take it and it won't be boxes of lead this time!"

"But, Captain, we've lost a lot of men, and these men aren't up for another fight!" complained the sergeant major.

"This is our last chance, Sergeant Major, now do as you're told!"

"Yessir!" responded the very reluctant sergeant as he turned to roust the men around.

Reuben was relieved to see the band of Confederates break camp, but he was surprised to see them turn back to the north. He chuckled as he realized what had prompted the change of plans, *They opened the boxes and now they're going back to find where the gold is, maybe to go after the freighters.* He continued to watch until they were out of sight beyond the low hills to the north, knowing they were definitely bound for the Overland Trail that paralleled the South Platte. With a glance to the sun, he guessed there was about three hours of daylight left, and chose to try for a couple hours' rest before they took to the trail.

He walked back to the camp, saw the girl wrapped in Elly's arms as they cuddled on the blanket in the shade of the big juniper, Micah had stretched out nearby and was partially wrapped in the other blanket. Reuben grinned, enjoying the sight, and having thoughts of a family of his own someday. He saw the coffeepot sitting near the coals of the cookfire and poured himself the last of it. He sat down next to the big rock, leaned back, and sipped the hot brew, looking at the rolling plains that stretched out to the north and east where they were bound. As he finished off the coffee, he tossed the dregs aside and sat the cup down, wiggled around a bit to make himself comfortable and was about to close his eyes when motion caught his attention.

Two men, afoot, were hugging the edge of the bluff, moving from sage to sage and drawing near their camp. Reuben rolled to the side, picked up his Henry and walked into the trees. As the men neared, he recognized them as two of the men from the two wagons, but with only two, there could be one or two more somewhere else. He watched the two men drop behind a big sage and decided to move to higher ground to see if the others were also nearby. He catfooted it between the juniper, moving alongside the edge of the rimrock to a point overlooking the camp and the surrounding area. His first look was to see the two men, who were trying to see into the camp and who was there; he could tell by their gestures they were wanting to get to the horses, but they could not without going through the camp. He made a quick survey of the outlying area, searching for any others, but there were none to be found.

Satisfied, he worked his way back closer to the camp, still hidden in the trees and watched. Elly and the youngsters were still asleep, and the men rose from behind the big rock to start toward the camp, one going to the trees, the other approaching from the clearing. Reuben usually kept a cartridge in the chamber of his Henry and now, as quietly as possible, eared back the hammer. One man stepped from the trees, carrying a rifle across his chest as he looked around, and noticing the woman and children, he began searching the trees for Reuben. He had taken another step when the first man walked into the camp from the clearing, also carrying a rifle.

"That's far enough!" declared Reuben, revealing himself with the rifle at his shoulder and aimed at the nearest man. "Drop 'em!" he demanded. He saw Elly roll from the blankets, pushing the girl behind the tree and knew she would have her pistol in hand.

The man furthest from Reuben started to lift his rifle, and Reuben dropped the hammer on him, the bullet taking him in the solar plexus, blossoming red and blowing out his backbone, dropping him in a heap. Instantly, Reuben jacked another cartridge into the chamber, but the first man had lifted his rifle and was pulling the trigger when Elly's pistol blasted. The bullet split the rifle stock at the man's cheek, burrowing a channel into the man's face and taking his nose with it. The man tried to scream, choked on it as he dropped to his knees, the barrel of the rifle driving into the ground as he pulled the trigger. The blast exploded the barrel, splitting it lengthwise and blowing a small crater in the dirt, just before the man's face was buried in the hole.

Silence fell like a blanket over the trees and the clearing as both Reuben and Elly stood still, glancing from one man to the other, then looking at one another. "Who are they?" she asked.

"They were from the two wagons that passed us and tried to rob us. Even after I helped them out of the mess they were in with the renegades, they still tried to steal our horses."

"That's gratitude for ya'!" declared Elly, shaking her head. She looked around, looked up at Reuben. "While you drag them outta here, I'll fix us something to eat before it gets dark, and we take to the trail."

"Sounds good. By the way, thanks for that shot, he was about to shoot me!"

Elly smiled. "That's getting to be a habit with me. You

149

might try being a little more careful, save me the trouble," she added, giggling as she spoke.

THE WESTERN SKY WAS A BRILLIANT DISPLAY OF GOLD AND orange when the small contingent of travelers emerged from the trees. Reuben led the way with Micah sitting on the bedroll behind the cantle, and the long lead kept the pack mule close behind. Elly nudged her blood sorrel beside Reuben, one arm around Mary's middle as she sat behind the pommel, crowding Elly in the seat but sitting tight. The lead for the second pack mule was loosely wrapped around the saddle horn and the pack mule sided the other one as the travelers started into the flats. The buffalo grass glowed orange with the setting sun behind them, as the shadows of the sage stretched before them. Reuben had, as usual, picked his landmark to mark their way, a single narrow tipped butte to the northeast that marred the otherwise flat vista of the rolling plains, the tip showing a brighter orange as the disappearing sun highlighted the anomaly.

They no longer followed a designated trail, cutting across the flats to make their way to the distant Overland Trail and the South Platte River. Although they had traveled through the country when they came out on the stage, this land was all new to them. Yet Reuben appreciated the vast wilderness of the plains, so different from the farmland of the Midwest that had been his childhood home. Back there at this time of year he remembered everything being thick with foliage and greenery, yet heavy with the humid heat. This land was wide open, the air thin, dry, and clear, and many times it was as if they could see forever. It was a wild land, and so were the people that he had come to know as Arapaho, Cheyenne,

Sioux, as well as the pioneers from the east that were settling this land.

The moon was well up in the eastern sky, its bold white face ready to take its place among the lights of the night and the curtain of dusk was snuffing out the colors of the sunset. Reuben's melancholy thoughts were interrupted when Micah spoke, "Reuben?"

"Yes, Micah."

"Is it always like this?"

"What do you mean?"

"I mean all this killin'. When we were on our way out, some Indians attacked and one of the women was killed. And then when we wanted to go back, well, you know what happened. And then, back there, those two men. Why?"

"That's a mighty hard question, Micah. But let me see if I can answer it for you. As far as the Indians attackin', well, they were mad about all the people comin' out from the east and takin' their homeland away, drivin' off the buffalo, and even killin' some of their own. The men in Washington, politicians they're called, had signed a treaty promisin' the white men would leave the Indians and their homes alone, stay away. But when gold was discovered, many people, like your Dad and the others with him, wanted some of that gold and didn't do as the treaty said. And the politicians had promised to pay the natives for their land, and they didn't. So you can see why they were upset and tried to drive the white men away, and it's still not settled.

"And those renegades that attacked your wagons and killed everybody, well, that was just greed and meanness. Evil men doin' evil things. You see, Micah, the Bible says *All have sinned and come short of the glory of God. (Rom. 3:23)* And *The wages of sin is death; but the gift of God is eternal live through Jesus Christ our Lord. (Rom. 6:23)* Have you ever done bad things, Micah?"

The boy nodded his head against Reuben's back and quietly admitted, "Yessir."

"We all have, Micah. But God says there is a penalty, which is death, but He also gives us a gift, so we don't have to pay that penalty. That gift is eternal life, purchased for us by Jesus on the cross. And all we have to do is accept that gift. He tells us that in Romans 10:9-10 *That if thou shalt confess with thy mouth the Lord Jesus and shalt believe in thine heart that God hath raised him from the dead, thou shalt be saved. For with the heart man believeth unto righteousness...* See, Micah, if we believe Him, and accept his gift of eternal life, then we will be saved. Then our heart will guide us to *righteousness,* or right livin'."

"Yeah, but *you* killed those men back there; was that right?"

"Sometimes, doin' right is not the easy thing to do. Just like in the Bible when David stood before the giant, Goliath. He had to kill the giant that wanted to kill all of his people. So, yes, he killed a man, but he did it to save many others. When I shot that man, he was about to kill Elly, and I couldn't allow that. And when she shot the other man, he was about to kill me. So, what we did was a terrible thing, in that we took a life, but we did it to save a life, and that is a good thing. Do you understand that, Micah?"

"I think so. I guess there will always be times when good people have to stand against bad people to keep bad things from happenin'."

"That's right. Remember, it's not always easy, but it is necessary."

. . .

WITH THE NORTH STAR QUARTERED OFF HIS LEFT shoulder, Reuben kept them on the trail to the northeast. With a brief stop just after midnight to give the animals a drink and some graze, they traveled through the night. The sun was slowly pushing back the curtain of darkness with its grey line of pale light when Reuben spotted the outlines of the buildings of what he thought was the Bijou Creek station. They knew they were near when the hard crusted soil showed the white alkali and stretches of soft sand; the nemesis of the stages. But the shadowy silhouettes that stood before them marked the station with the two single story log buildings backed by the big barn and the large corral.

As they neared, Reuben called out, "Ho the barn! Alright if we come in?"

A hostler stuck his head out the door to look at the visitors, motioning them in as he answered, "Come ahead on! Everybody else is here, you might as well join us!"

Reuben frowned as he neared the buildings, remembering it a bit different and turned to the hostler, "Is this Bijou Creek?"

The hostler chuckled. "If you was aimin' fer Bijou, you done missed it by 'bout eighteen mile. This hyar is Beaver Creek!"

Reuben shook his head, but pleased they were further east that he hoped, and Beaver Creek was a home station that would offer meals to the travelers. Plus, it would save them about a half day's travel. It was common for travelers to find refuge in the stations, both for their animals and themselves and as Reuben and Elly showed themselves in the dim light, the hostler, a colored man, stood watching, grinning, as he asked, "You got young'uns wit'chu?"

"Two of 'em, and they're sayin' they are hungry. They gonna have breakfast in yonder?" asked Reuben, nodding toward the main building as he slipped his leg over the pommel and neck of his horse to slide to the ground. He reached for Micah and helped him to the ground as the hostler answered, "If you wanna call it that, they do," chuckling.

"Anythin' we don't hafta build a fire for will suit us just fine." He looked around, saw the two hostlers were busy harnessing teams for the stage and Reuben asked, "That'n headin' west or east?"

The hostler chuckled. "This'ns goin' west, but the east bound'll be comin' thru in 'bout an hour or so. But they had a little trouble back up the line, so they might be a little late. You gonna give up horses for a coach seat?"

Reuben grinned. "Uh, nope. Just wonderin'."

With a nod to Elly, he motioned for her to take the youngsters into the station while he tended to their animals. Reuben looked to the hostler as Elly left. "Got a few stalls for our animals?"

"Sure, gonna cost ya' though."

"That's alright. We been ridin' all night and they need some rest, and if it's alright with you, we'll bed down beside 'em."

"That'll be fine, but what with all the coaches comin' an' goin', you might not get much rest out'chere."

"Prob'ly get less in the bunkhouse," resolved Reuben, stabling the animals.

After giving them water, Reuben rubbed down the horses and the mules, and put some grain in the manger for the weary travelers. With the tack and panniers stacked in a separate stall, he lay out the bedrolls in preparation of a good day's rest. A familiar voice asked, "You plannin' on sleepin' a week?"

Reuben turned to see a smiling Levi and Whiskers standing at the end of the stall. They laughed as Reuben broke into a grin and stepped to the men to shake the hands of the old friends. "It is good to see you!" with a glance to Levi's bandaged middle, he asked, "What's that all about?"

"Ah, we got jumped by a bunch o' Confederate deserters or sumpin'. They was a bad bunch, but ol' Myrtle put one o' 'em down, yessiree!"

"Did they get anything?" asked Reuben, trying to be nonchalant but curious.

"Yeah, they got a couple strongboxes that was s'posed to have gold in 'em, but we don't know fer sure. Seems some marshal back in Denver did a little switcheroo and ain't nobody whut knows where the real strongboxes went," explained Whiskers.

"So, when did all this happen?"

"Yestiddy mornin'," replied Levi, looking at Reuben with a bit of a frown that had a question mark written across his expression.

Reuben stuck his foot on the lower board of the stable sidewall, his elbow on the top, as he looked at Levi and pointed with his chin to the bandage. "So, I reckon with that you'll be laid up a day or two?"

"Bof of us will. We go together where'er we go, so this gits us bof a couple days off," he answered, grinning, and glanced at Whiskers.

"Then let's go get us some breakfast," suggested Reuben, starting toward the door. The two men fell in beside him and Whiskers said, "We already ate, but we'll drink some coffee with you. By the way, where'd you get them young'uns?"

"Oh, picked 'em up back yonder a ways."

"What'cha gonna do with 'em?" asked Levi.

"Dunno. But it'll come to us I reckon."

They were enjoying their breakfast when a ruckus in the yard brought everyone out of the log building. The line of freighters limped into the station, some with four mules, others with the usual six-up. Atop the second freighter lay three bodies, and several of the other men sported bandages. The wagon boss, Henry Hatcher, jumped down from the seat of the first wagon and began to shout orders to the teamsters to line the freighters out near the barn to unload the supplies. Once they were situated, he turned toward the station, saw Reuben, walked closer and said, "Them rebel deserters or whatever they were sure tried their best, but we let 'em have it! Don't think they were expectin' us to circle up like we done and when our men returned fire from atop those tall wagons, we cut 'em down like harvestin' wheat! There was only 'bout a dozen of 'em, but after we saw the graves of the sojer boys and talked to the captain, we was expectin' 'em. Had outriders that saw 'em comin' so we circled up and waited." He popped his galluses, grinning and laughing, "Their eyes were bigger'n their weapons, we prob'ly dropped half of 'em 'fore they turned tail and skedaddled! We didn't hang around to bury 'em, what with the cargo we're carryin'." He gave a big wink to Reuben to assure him the cargo was safe. He turned on his heel and added over his shoulder, "Gotta get them supplies unloaded and get back on the road!"

Levi and Whiskers looked at Reuben, with a glance to the retreating wagon boss, and back to Reuben when Levi said, "If'n I didn't know better, it sure seemed to me like he was reportin' in to you! He weren't doin' that, right?"

"Now why would he do that? He prob'ly just saw a familiar face, we met him in Denver city at the company office, and had to tell somebody." answered Reuben, shrugging. "But boys, I think you'll have to excuse us, we need to get some sleep. We been travelin' all night and that stall, and my blankets are callin' me!" He put his arm around Elly and motioned to the youngsters to come along as he steered them toward the barn and the stall with their bedding.

As they walked away, Levi and Whiskers looked at one another, Levi with one eyebrow cocked up and he said to his partner, "There's more to that boy than we know."

"Ummhmm, I'm thinkin' you're right about that," answered Whiskers, "but there's some coffee left and we don't want it to get throwed out, so..." he suggested as he turned to go back inside the eating room.

DUSK HAD RETREATED, DRAGGING ITS CURTAIN OF DIM light with it, and the heavenly bodies had lit their lanterns to decorate the velvety black of the endless sky. The big moon stood off the right shoulder of the travelers that kept their distance from the well-traveled road of the Overland Trail. It was not until the trail broke from the Oregon Trail to loop to the south that its name was changed from the Platte River Trail to the Overland Trail, due to the coaches of the Overland Stage that branded the plains with the hard packed two track called a road. Although the trail sided the South Platte, it usually rode about a hundred yards away, leaving room for the many wagon trains and freight trains to camp near the water, but Reuben shied well away from the busy camps of wagons and freighters, preferring to pass unnoticed.

They passed Kelly's Station, or the American Ranch, right at the fall of dusk and a couple of the stock hands waved as they passed. But darkness obscured their passing between Godfrey's Station and the thickets of the river, making them appear as just another shadow in the darkness. Valley Station was a telegraph office and lights were burning in the windows of the buildings as Reuben and company passed by unnoticed. The cool air of the night kept the youngsters huddled up to their keepers and the easy gait of the horses rocked them to sleep, allowing the night sounds of crickets, cicadas, coyotes, and owls to provide a lullaby to keep them at rest.

A wide stretch of emptiness and the inviting clearing

in the trees beside the river tempted Reuben to stop for a brief rest for the horses and a stretch for the riders. After loosening the girths of the animals, Reuben tethered them within reach of a shallow backwater of the river and a wide stretch of graze. He returned to Elly's side for a handful of smoked meat as they stretched out, leaning against a downed cottonwood with the youngsters by their side.

Elly looked at Reuben as they worked on the tough smoked meat and asked, "Do you think we could stop by to see Sadie and Mabel?"

Reuben frowned as he remembered the girls Elly spoke of and chuckled at the memory. They were the two girls taken captive by the Cheyenne Dog Soldiers and Reuben and Elly had done a little trading with the leader of the raiding band, Tall Bull, trading him a 'far-shooting rifle' for the girls. After returning the young women to their ranch, they spent some time with them before accepting the assignment with the stage line. Their ranch was north of Dennison's Ranch, a station for the stage line, but on the far side of the river.

"If we push it a little, we might get there in time for breakfast!" he answered with a droll.

She smiled as she playfully slapped his arm. "You were already planning on stopping, weren't you?!"

"Prob'ly," he answered, chuckling, and laughing at his playful woman.

Micah and Mary were listening and watching the two and Micah asked, "Do they have any kids?"

"No, but there's two ladies that love to cook good food for hungry visitors! Do you like flapjacks?"

Micah smiled and wiggled a little. "Boy! Do I! So does Mary!"

"Then we will try to get there in time for breakfast!

Sound good?" asked Reuben, bending down to look directly at little Mary.

"Ummhmm," answered the usually bashful Mary, smiling and nodding.

"Then we better take care of the necessaries," suggested Reuben. "Boys downstream, girls upstream!" he declared, "And take your rifle, Elly."

"Always do, if for no other reason than to rescue you!" she declared.

Reuben and Micah had gone into the trees, following a faint trail in the dim moonlight, when Reuben smelled something and reached down a hand to stop Micah, putting his finger to his lips to silence the boy. Reuben went to one knee, motioned Micah to do the same, and began searching the scattered trees and willows for movement. But it was a shadow on a high branch of a tangled cottonwood that caught his eye. He looked up to see a ball of black fur huddled against the trunk and looking below. Reuben dropped his eyes to see a big mama black bear playfully cuffing another cub about the ears. Reuben nodded toward the scene for Micah to see, but the boy had already spotted the playful trio and was staring wide-eyed. The bears were about twenty yards away and Reuben felt the slight breeze, relieved to know that he and the boy were upwind of the furry family. They watched until the cub came down from the tree and the mother led them away, further downstream, looking for berries and such for their supper. They would forage most of the night, and sleep most of the day.

As they returned to the camp, the girls were also returning and an enthusiastic and excited Micah said, "Guess what we saw! A mama bear and her two cubs!

They were close, too; the one cub was up in a tree and the other'n was playin' with his mama!"

Mary looked at Elly. "Can we go see?"

"They're long gone now, kiddo," declared Reuben, frowning when he looked at Elly who was holding something in her arms. "What'chu got there?"

Elly smiled and opened her arms a little to reveal a ball of black fur with two shiny black eyes and tuft of white at its throat. "I heard it whimpering in the willows and picked it up. It kinda looks like a wolf, but I think it's more dog. Maybe it got left behind by some wagons."

"What're you gonna do with a pup?"

"Now that's a silly question to ask a woman, don't'cha think?" she snickered, smiling.

The skeleton of a new barn caught the morning sun making the new lumber shine white. Reuben nodded. "Looks like the Cash brothers have been workin' right along."

Elly grinned, remembering the two brothers that had been courting the two girls they rescued from the Cheyenne Dog Soldiers and the way they bickered about the marriage-minded girls. "At least they've been doing something besides fighting one another."

"They'll prob'ly finish that in a week or so, I didn't expect them to have it done until closer to fall."

"Ah, they're good men, just need a little growing up and maybe a loving hand to guide them."

Reuben shook his head. "There ya go again. You women just can't stand to see an eligible male that's unmarried."

They rode into the big yard before the ranch house, greeted by the scruffy lop-eared dog that seldom left the porch and the screen door creaked open and Sadie shouted, "Elly! Reuben!" as she vaulted down the steps to run to Elly's side, stopped and frowned at the sight of the little girl, looked to the boy behind Reuben, and chuckled as she said, "You two didn't waste any time!" laughing. "Come on and get down, everyone's in the house and Ma's fixing breakfast. She's gonna be glad to see you two!"

Sadie caught Dustan Cash's eye and motioned for him to take the horses to the barn, but Reuben held up his hand to stay the young man and explained, "I'll take care of the animals. I want to rub them down and take care of the gear. Is it alright if I make a place in the stalls for our bedrolls?"

"You'll do no such thing! We have a spare room inside and you'll be staying there!" declared Sadie, brokering no argument as she took Elly's arm to escort her and the youngsters into the house. The ladies swarmed around the youngsters and Elly, anxious to hear the story of what appeared to be her rapidly growing family and with the kitchen already crowded, they ushered her to a seat at the table, but Ethel called from the kitchen, speaking for her and Mabel, "We want to hear this too! Can you wait a bit?"

"Of course, that is if I can get a cup of coffee!" answered Elly, laughing as the others.

While the ladies were busy in the house, Dustan and Jeremiah joined Reuben and gave him a hand with the rubdowns of the animals. The gear was stacked in a spare stall that lined out with the others in the lean-to addition of the barn, the only portion that had a roof and siding and provided all the protection needed for the animals and the gear. As Dustan rubbed down one of the pack mules, he looked at Reuben. "So, did you have yourself quite an adventure with your trip to Denver City?"

"Depends on what you mean by adventure. If you

mean was there excitement, fightin', and such like, yeah, there was plenty of that!"

"So, was it all in Denver?" asked Jeremiah, pausing as he brushed Elly's sorrel mare and looking over her back at Reuben.

"No, not much happened in Denver City, too many people! Now, we fought some Indians on the way to Denver, had a little ruckus with some scalawags in Latham. Then we had a run-in with some go-backers and another one with some renegades and a bunch of rag-tag Indians on the way here. But that's about all. Just enough to keep us from gettin' bored."

Jeremiah looked to his brother and back to Reuben. "Sure don't sound borin' to me! Mite dangerous, but not borin'!"

"You gonna be able to stay around long or are you off to some other adventure?" asked Dustan.

"Well, I do need to ride on into Julesburg, meet with Holladay. But after that, might head west to the mountains! Didn't get to see them close up this time, and I'm thinkin' I'd kinda like to do that."

"Now that sounds like somethin' to my likin'," declared Jeremiah, seeing Dustan nod his head in agreement.

"But aren't you two talkin' marriage sometime soon?" asked Reuben, grinning.

Both brothers lifted their heads to look over the back of the animals with wide eyes at Reuben, "Who you been talkin' to?" blurted Dustan.

"In case you didn't know it, that's about all women talk about, either gettin' married, or gettin' one or more of their friends married. All those women in the house yonder, I'd be willin' to bet my last dollar that they're plannin' a couple weddin's right now!" chuckled

Reuben, finishing his job of rubbing down his steel dust.

The brothers were speechless and busied themselves with the brushing, shaking their heads as confused thoughts ran through their minds. Both had talked about getting married someday, and the likelihood of marrying Sadie and Mabel had been a part of those discussions, but in their minds, 'someday' was a long way off.

Jeremiah finished first and walked around behind the mule, careful to keep his hand on the animal's rump so he would know what was happening, and came near Reuben. "You really think that's what they're doin'?"

Reuben grinned, nodding. "Ummhmm. But what's wrong with that? Both of you are old enough, and you've got a good job, and there would probably be a place for you to put up a cabin here at the ranch. That wouldn't be so bad, would it?"

"But, but, I was thinkin' like sometime in the future, you know, maybe a year or two down the road. Not now!" he declared, twisting his face into a contorted mask of distaste and discomfort as he sat down on the edge of the haymow, shaking his head.

"Why wait? Married life is alright. Me'n Elly are doin' fine."

"But that's different!"

"Why?"

He groaned as he shook his head. "I dunno, just is, that's all."

"Yeah," came a weak rejoinder from Dustan.

"Fellas, it's like this. If you think you love 'em, and you can see yourselves together for the rest of your lives, then don't wait. I've seen too much to know that you can't always count on tomorrow, and if you wait, it might be too late. If I remember right, when we were here before and we went to that dance, there were quite a few other fellas that were wantin' to dance with those girls."

"Yeah, you're right about that, and we've talked about it, but..." answered Jeremiah, shrugging, and looking to his brother. But Dustan had nothing to say.

"Well, I'm gettin' hungry! You fellas have breakfast yet?"

"Nope!" declared Jeremiah, putting a smile on his face as he stood to join Reuben as they went to the house for the promised breakfast.

IT WAS WELL AFTER THE MIDDAY MEAL BEFORE REUBEN, Elly and the youngsters were able to get some time away to catch up on some shuteye. They were tired after riding all night and could barely hold their heads up when Mable ushered them all into the spare room, where pallets had been made on the floor for the children and the bed was ready for Reuben and Elly. Weariness soon took over and the four were enjoying the best sleep they had in several days.

Hunger brought Reuben awake as the smells of cooking drifted in from the kitchen and as he stirred, so did the others. Elly was drowsy until a cold, wet nose touched her neck. She twisted around to see her recently acquired ball of black fur smiling at her with wide eyes as he laid his chin on her neck. She giggled and drew the big pup close to scratch behind his ears and laugh at his playful antics. "You are a scruffy one, aren't you?"

Everyone came for the evening meal and the conversation picked up where it left off, but when the subject of marriage was broached, the brothers became uncomfortable and coughed and squirmed until Reuben said,

"Well ladies, this has been an enjoyable visit, but we need to finish our journey to Julesburg! We'll be leavin' about dusk, but hopefully, we'll be comin' back in a day or two, if that would be alright?"

"Riding at night? Is it safe?" asked Ethel, Sadie's mother.

Elly chimed in, "We find it much safer to travel at night. Most of the natives are in their camps, outlaws are too lazy to get out after dark, and with a big moon and a clear night, it's quite pleasant!"

"Well, you make it sound lovely!" replied Mabel's mother, Gladys. Both women had recently struggled when their daughters had been taken by the Cheyenne Dog Soldiers and the nights brought nothing but wild imaginations and fear.

"I need to be in Julesburg first thing, and after we tend to a little business, swap horses and such, we'll be back on the road west," explained Reuben.

CAPTAIN MADISON WAS ANGERED AS MUCH BY THE damage to his uniform as he was with the flesh wound to his shoulder. One of the bullets from the muleskinners burned a furrow across his shoulder, ripping the epaulet and covering the back with blood. But the wound, coupled with their failure to get the gold, had filled him with rage. He was not a man that took defeat and failure well, for those were experiences he had not tolerated. Nor was he willing to admit defeat this time, even with the loss of most of his command.

He stomped back and forth before the remains of his company of volunteers. "Crocket! You will take your two men, you're familiar with the stage stations and such, and ride for all you're worth to get to Julesburg before any gold shipment! Check with each of the stations to see if there is any news about the gold and if there is anything worthy, send a telegram to any station along the way. You should overtake the freighters so you can watch when they unload and such; find that gold!"

He drove his fist into his palm. "I'll take the rest of the men, we'll split up and all be in civies, and follow behind the freighters, unless we discover anything different! The stage driver and shotgunner we hit should be somewhere along the way, and they will have said something about when they were hit. Also, the freighters would have said something. But if there is nothing certain about the gold, keep riding until you get to Julesburg! Change horses at any ranch you come to!" he tossed a bag of gold coin to him. "That'll keep you in fresh horses. Don't stop!"

Crocket nodded to the captain, turned to his two scruffy men, Stink and Baldy, and motioned with his chin for them to mount up. He swung aboard his mount and without a backward glance to the others, dug heels to his horse's ribs and the three left at a full gallop, determined to do the captain's bidding, or maybe just find the gold, whatever was the most profitable.

"You know, we've got a little chestnut mare out there that is as sweet as she can be, and I'm thinking a couple of youngsters would be great company for her, maybe take her for a ride," suggested Sadie as she sat beside the two little ones.

Micah was wide-eyed as he listened, and Mary tapped her on the leg to get her attention and asked, "Is she little 'nuff for me?"

Sadie chuckled a little, nodding. "Yes, she's little 'nuff for you. She's been a part of this ranch almost as long as I have, and she loves little ones! And we have another one, a little bigger, that would be just right for your brother!" as she looked over at Micah. She looked to Elly, "Since you two are going to be coming back this way anyway, you might just let these two stay with us and have a little fun while you're gone!"

"Are you sure? We hadn't thought about that. They have an Uncle back in Missouri and we were considering putting them on a stage to go back to their family."

Micah dropped his head and mumbled, "He's mean!"

"What? Did you say he's mean? Why would you say that?" asked Elly, frowning.

Micah squirmed, looked at Mary and then to Elly. "He beats his kids with a whip, makes them do all the work and he goes to town to drink whiskey."

Elly frowned, looking at Micah to determine how serious he was, glanced to Reuben and back to Sadie. "We didn't know that," she answered, then looking at Reuben. "Maybe it would be good to send a telegram to his family, tell them what happened and see what they want to do." She looked at Sadie, shaking her head. "I'd hate to send them back into a bad situation where they wouldn't be loved or allowed to be kids."

"Then it's settled, they'll stay with us while you two go to Julesburg to tend to your business and find out about their family." She turned to Micah and Mary, "Would you like to stay with us?"

Micah smiled and asked, "Will there be more flapjacks?"

Gladys and Ethel laughed as they looked at one another and answered together, "You bet there will!"

THE MOON WAS WANING FROM FULL AND HUNG HIGH IN the eastern sky as the other heavenly bodies lit their lanterns at random, making the moon appear as a mother hen gathering her wayward chicks. They kept to the two-track trail on the north side of the river, a trail made by the different ranchers' buckboards making frequent supply trips to Julesburg. Across the black ribbon that marked the foliage and bed of the South Platte, the Overland Trail showed like a thin string paralleling the winding river. Cookfires of a wagon train camped near the river flickered like candles on a birthday cake, but they knew the weary travelers were not celebrating anything.

All the stage stations were on the south side of the Platte, and they saw the lights of Dennison's Ranch shimmering in the station and barn, shadows passing to and fro, busy about their duties. While the south side had the sand hills, alkali and rolling flats, the north side had bunch grass, sage, rabbit brush and more. Several ranches dotted the flats between the river and the low mesas, buttes, and finger ridges. Most were what some would call two by four outfits, two buildings, usually one dug out, and maybe four cows. Within a handful of years, they would be swallowed up by the bigger ranches or left to deteriorate, and the settlers would add their graves to those on the south side.

They rode side by side, each one trailing a pack mule, and with the pup riding in her lap Elly asked about the constellations and how to tell directions by the stars. Reuben grinned, pointed out the constellation known as Ursa Major. "That one's known as the big bear, or some call it the big dipper. See how it looks like a big water dipper some folks have at their wells?"

"Oh, I see it. I've seen that before but didn't know it as the big bear. Why do they call it the big bear?"

"Well, the first two stars of the handle are the tail of the bear, and the dipper and those three stars to the right of it, form the body of the bear, and those stars below the dipper and the front, are the legs. There's a lot of different ideas about the bear, some say the handle is actually his neck and head, others have him upside down, but what I showed you is the most popular."

"But how do I find my way at night?"

Reuben grinned, nodded back to the big bear. "See those two stars at the edge of the big dipper?" and looked at Elly as she nodded. "Use those two to draw a straight line and that will take you to the north star. If you look closely, you'll see that is the star at the end of the handle of the Little Dipper, or Polaris. The North Star is always there, and when you know North, you can figure out any direction you need. So, with that being North, which way are we goin'?"

Elly frowned, turned to face directly at the star, held her arms out to the side and looked down the road that was quartered between her chin and her right shoulder, then answered, "Northeast!"

Reuben smiled and nodded. "Good! That's exactly right. But maybe I made a mistake tellin' you all that," as he frowned a little, looking sideways at his wife.

"Why?"

"Now that you have your directions, you'll probably be wantin' to tell me where to go!"

She leaned over and slapped his shoulder, giggling. "Oh you!"

It was close to midnight when they took to the trees near the river for a breather for the horses and some rest for the riders. Reuben dug a shallow hole, built a hat sized fire in the hole and stacked rocks around it to shield it from view while Elly filled the coffeepot and put it on the nearest rock. While it was heating, she ground some coffee beans on a flat rock beside the fire and within moments the pot was dancing, and she dropped in a small handful of fresh ground coffee. Once it began to boil, she gave it a few moments, pulled it away from the fire and poured in a bit of cold water to settle the grounds, and poured them each a cup of steaming brew. Reuben quickly covered the fire with dirt, avoiding the smell and smoke of a doused fire and sat back to enjoy the coffee and the smoked meat in the company of his woman.

"What have you been thinking about the children?" asked Elly, looking up at her man.

Reuben shook his head. "I dunno. After what Micah said, that makes it difficult. They should be with family, but sometimes family is not always best. It would be different if it was, oh, maybe a grandparent or such, but a drinkin' uncle that mistreats his own kids, that's different."

"But what do we do if we don't send them back to Missouri?"

"I dunno. I kinda got attached to 'em both. That Micah's smarter'n a whip and always eager to help and learn; he's a good kid, and so is Mary. She has a rare quality for a girl."

"What's that?"

Reuben chuckled. "She's unusually quiet!"

Elly shook her head. "You are incorrigible!"

Both laughed, but the sounds of several animals crossing the river alarmed them, and Reuben snatched up his Henry and went to the edge of the trees. A quick glance back to the camp told him they were well hidden, and he moved to a big snag of a cottonwood that stood like a lone sentinel at the edge of the trees. About fifty yards downstream, several horses came from the river, some ridden, others being driven. Even from this distance he could tell this was a raiding band of natives, probably young bucks out to prove themselves, that had stolen the horses either from a ranch, a stage station, or a camp of would-be gold hunters. He watched and guessed at the number of horses and raiders, settling on about a dozen or more driven horses, and eight or ten raiders.

He made no move to stop them but stayed obscured as the band drove their bounty away from the river toward the distant buttes and draws. Within a short while, they were swallowed by the black maw of a deep draw that split the flat top mesas to the northwest.

Elly had come beside him and asked, "Who do you think they were?"

"Had to be Cheyenne. Most of the Arapaho are south of the river."

"Dog Soldiers?"

"Prob'ly not. I'm guessin' they were young bucks out to prove themselves. Stealin' horses is a good way to gain honors, be accepted into a warrior society like the Dog Soldiers."

As they started to turn back to their camp, another ruckus of horses crossing the shallows of the river caught their attention. They watched a handful of riders come from the trees, obviously white men following the raiders, but there was only five or six of them. As they broke from the trees, one of the men directed the others to split up, some going upstream, some down, apparently searching for the trail of the raiders. Although the horse thieves had ridden straight from the river, the hard ground of the rocky flats and the hard packed trail, made trailing in the dark a challenge, but it also showed the inexperience of the group.

Reuben stepped from the trees to show himself and the three that came his direction were busy looking at the ground and didn't see him till they almost rode him down. The leader of the group reined up. "Hey! Who're you? What're you doin' here?"

"I could ask you the same question, but it's obvious you're lookin' for the trail of your stolen horses."

"How'd you know?"

"I saw 'em come from the river just a little bit ago."

"Why didn't you stop 'em?" growled one of the other men. "They was Injuns an' you're a white man!"

"You noticed that, didja?"

The mouthy man slapped legs to his mount and lunged him toward Reuben, attempting to run him over, but Reuben deftly stepped aside, driving the butt of his rifle up under the chin of the belligerent man, unseating him and dropping him on his back with a thump that knocked his air out. The two others started to move against Reuben, but he brought the muzzle of the rifle around toward them and cautioned, "Might not wanna do that!"

Both men reined up and sat easy, watching their friend squirm around on the ground, gasping for air and trying to get up. He sat up, looked at Reuben and his friends, slowly rising to his feet, feeling his jaw, and shaking his head as he glowered at Reuben. "Where's muh horse?" he asked his friends and one of the men moved off to fetch the man's animal that stood a ways off in the sage, munching on some gramma. The man looked at Reuben again and repeated his question, "Like I said before, why didn't you stop 'em?"

"Wasn't my affair. Not my horses, not my problem."

The man turned at the sound of the rest of his group riding up just as his horse was returned and as he grabbed the reins of his mount, he looked at the others and reported, "This," and stammered for a description of his opinion of Reuben, settling on, "fool watched our horses be driven by them thievin' Injuns and didn't do nuthin' 'bout it!"

The leader, a big barrel-chested man with thick whiskers, glared at Reuben and asked, "Why not?"

"Didn't want to," answered Reuben, his Henry

cradled in his arms and turning slightly so the muzzle was directed at the new threat.

"You got horses?" asked the leader, scowling.

"I didn't walk here!"

"Oh, a wiseacre, huh? Well, we'll just see about that!"

Reuben stepped back slightly, bringing the muzzle of the rifle to bear on the big man and said, "Only if you want to be buried here!" That stopped the leader, and Reuben added, "Your horses were taken by a band of Cheyenne. They were young bucks out to prove them-selves and by now they are back at their village. There's probably a hundred warriors, most of them proven Dog Soldiers, some of the fiercest fightin' men of the plains, and if you go ridin' in there, you won't ride out! The best thing you can do is forget the horses, hitch up your wagons and get on down the trail."

One of the other men answered, "Maybe we oughta just take his horses and leave him afoot!"

A couple of the others agreed with the suggestion adding their brief remarks until Reuben shot the hat off the man that made the suggestion and instantly jacked another shell into his Henry. "In case you didn't know it, stealin' a man's horse in this country is a hangin' offense. And if you try to steal mine, you won't live long enough to hang!"

To emphasize his point, another shot came from the trees, piercing the darkness, and the dirt at the feet of the leader's horse kicked up and startled the animal, setting him to bucking and snorting. The greenhorn was doing his best to hold on, but the horse tried to paw the stars, bent in the middle and put his face between his front feet and kicked at the moon with his rear feet, launching his rider face first into a big stand of greasewood. All the others had watched and moved away from the bucking horse; their own horses jittery at the display. When the big man rolled in the dirt away from the greasewood, his face and arms showing scratches and cuts, the sleeves of his shirt torn, and his countenance showing anger, he scrambled to his feet but was staring at the muzzle of Reuben's rifle just beyond his reach but the barrel looking mighty big. His eyes grew wide as he stuttered, "What'cha gonna do with that thing?"

"Now, that's entirely up to you."

"Careful, Bull, that shot came from the trees, we don't know how many there are!" cautioned one of his men, still trying to control his skittish horse.

"Alright, mister," began the big man, both hands raised high as he started backing away from Reuben, "you win this round. We'll leave." He glanced over his shoulder. "One o' you get my horse!"

As the men rode back toward the river crossing, their mumbling and complaining could be heard, and Reuben did not move from his place until he heard them cross the stream. He walked back to camp where a grinning Elly waited and he gave her a big hug. "Thanks darlin'. This is gettin' to be a habit with you, ain't it?"

"Good thing, too!" she replied, as they walked to their horses. Within just a few moments, the girths were tightened, the coffeepot packed, and they were on their way, anxious to put a few miles between them and the disgruntled wannabe gold seekers.

"For a while there I thought you were gonna have to shoot a few of 'em just to get them to pay attention to you!" commented Elly, looking to Reuben.

"That was the last thing I wanted to do, but..." and he left the thought of the possibility hang in the air between them.

25 /FAMILIAR FOES

T he steady rocking gait of the horses often gave a
sense of comfort and quiet, and blended the
nearby sounds of creaking leather, clomping of hooves
in the deep dusty trail, and the occasional snort of the
horses or mules. But the two travelers were accompa-
nied by the choir of the night, cicadas and crickets
providing the percussion, the bullfrogs and loons
carrying the melody, the nighthawks on high soprano,
and the occasional boom of the bass coming from the
great horned owl high in the cottonwoods. It was a
pleasant ride for the two travelers that were growing a
little sleepy, until a contrasting tune came from a distant
coyote stretching his narrow nose to the stars and crying
for his lost love. The black ball of fur in Elly's lap came
alive, lifting his head and looking around at the nearby
dark shadows, then back up at Elly with a questioning
expression on his fuzzy face that was accented by the
lone patch of white at his throat. Elly smiled and spoke
softly to the pup as she stroked his head and neck, "It's
alright boy, just a scrawny coyote looking for love."

But the coyote was answered by the clarion howl of a wolf from somewhere across the low hills to the north. The pup looked toward the howl, huddled closer to Elly, and looked at her with wide eyes as he trembled in her arms. Again, she comforted the pup, but this time she looked at Reuben. "He acts like he recognized the howl of that wolf! He's trembling!"

"He might remember somethin', maybe it's his daddy, or maybe it was a wolf that made him an orphan!" suggested Reuben. He stood in his stirrups and looked at the low hills to the north and west, then turned to look at the shadows of the river and the rolling hills beyond. He could see the ghostly forms of the Antelope Station, which was nothing more than a big barn, corrals and a two-room cabin. The swing stations had little accommodations for travelers and usually just catered to the teams, swapping them out as quickly as possible to send the coaches on their way with little delay. No lights showed, but the moonlight offered enough to make out the structures and the many animals in the corrals.

He looked at Elly. "That's Antelope Station yonder, so, we should get into Julesburg 'bout daylight. I dunno 'bout you, but I'm kinda lookin' forward to gettin' rid of these," he commented, taking the marshal's badge from his pocket.

Elly chuckled. "Why? They haven't left our pockets since we got 'em!"

"Just the same, too much responsibility," he explained nodding toward the mules.

"Ummhmm, but we'll be getting rid of that real soon now."

The closer they drew to Julesburg, the flat plains and low mesas were giving way to rolling hills that offered

179

deep shadows in the draws and wider vistas atop the hills. These hills rose as much as a hundred feet higher than the flats, and the lower swales often held juniper and piñon that drove their roots deep in the moist soil between the hills. The two-track road wound its way through the hills, keeping to the low ground, and as they neared Julesburg, they came to the river crossing that had prompted the original settlement to spring up where it now lay, on the south side of the river.

The eastern sky was showing grey and the low cloud cover and haze from the previous day's rainfall masked the rising sun, making it appear as a red ball hiding behind a wispy grey curtain. They splashed across the gravelly bottomed crossing, the slow current and shallow water giving the animals a drink without having to slow their progress. As they climbed the low bank, the horses shook off the excess, making Elly grab for the saddle horn to keep her grip on the pup who had stood with front feet on the pommel, one on either side of the horn and he almost lost his footing but was saved by Elly who giggled at his uncertainty.

The main road through town showed a warehouse and blacksmith shop that sandwiched the stage station between, with the stable on the far side of the blacksmith and big corrals behind. The opposite side held a hotel, general store that also had a tavern, a restaurant, a dress-maker, and a post office. A few houses were beyond the businesses, but most homes were behind the east side of the businesses. The town was slowly coming awake, someone was working the long handle of a pump that squealed for oil, fetching his morning water, a lop-eared dog lifted his head for a quick look at the passersby but soon dropped his head back between his paws, disinterested. A storekeeper was sweeping off the boardwalk in front of the general store and paused to look at the early arrivals, then continued his task. An old man, long grey beard covering his chest, was facing the rising sun, eyes closed, as he slowly pushed the rocker back and forth. Somewhere a screen door slapped at its frame as someone let it slip.

Reuben spoke quietly to Elly, "Let's go to the eatery there," pointing with a nod of his head, "we can tether the animals out front and sit by the window while we have us some breakfast. It doesn't look like there's anybody at the stage station yet, anyway."

"Sounds fine to me. I think Buster will stay here," she said, patting the pommel of the saddle.

"Buster?"

"Yeah. I think that fits him, don't you?"

"I reckon, but right now I'm cravin' some biscuits and gravy, how 'bout you?"

Elly smiled, nodded, and nudged the sorrel to the hitchrail and swung down, putting her hand on the pup so he would lay still on the seat of her saddle. Satisfied, she loosely wrapped the rein around the hitchrail, stepped under the sorrel's neck and tethered the mule. Reuben did the same with his animals and they stepped up on the boardwalk just as the door to the restaurant swung open and a smiling grey-haired woman stepped out, broom in hand and said, "Welcome folks! Comin' for breakfast, are ya?"

"You bet!" answered Reuben, reaching for Elly to come close. "We been ridin' a spell and I've been thinkin' 'bout hot biscuits and gravy. Please tell me you have some."

The woman smiled. "Best biscuits and gravy and all the rest of the fixin's you'll find for miles around! The only ones too!" she declared, laughing. "Go right on in folks, the girl there will take your order and get you some fresh coffee."

They were the first ones into the restaurant, the town's only eatery, and they took the table by the window. Elly looked out at the horses, smiled, and said, "Buster's stretched out in the seat and looks like he's dozing."

Reuben smiled, nodding, and added, "I'm lookin' forward to gettin' Blue back. That steel dust is a good horse, but me'n Blue, well, we just fit." He looked a little wistful as he thought of the horse he had for a good while before their journey to Denver City by stage.

"And I'm looking forward to seeing my Appy. I agree with you that little sorrel is a fine horse, but like you, I'm kinda partial to that Appy that Running Antelope and Wind in Her Hair gave me for a wedding present. She has such a smooth gait."

A young woman, her hair stacked high and her apron showing ruffles, stepped close and started pouring coffee into two cups, and with a broad smile, looked at the two and asked, "Is there something special you would like for breakfast?"

Reuben smiled but nodded to Elly to let her order first and she smiled at the waitress. "Yes, I'll have two eggs, sunny side up, potatoes, bacon, and biscuits."

"And you?" she asked, looking at Reuben.

"I'll have what she's havin' but add more biscuits and gravy."

The waitress smiled and turned away as she said, "It will be right out!"

While they waited, several townspeople came into the restaurant, greeting the women and each other, glancing toward Reuben and Elly and recognizing them as strangers to their town. Occasionally someone nodded, or even offered a "good morning", but most just found their seats and focused on their own business for the day.

"Are we going to head back to the Slade Ranch today?" asked Elly, casually looking out the window at the town that was slowly coming awake in the morning sun.

"Oh, I dunno. It might be nice to relax a bit, maybe get a room in the hotel and head back in the mornin'. You got anythin' you need to get while we're in town?"

"Nope. We got pretty well outfitted in Denver City."

Once the meal arrived, they gave all their attention to the plates full of delightful items they did not always get to enjoy on the trail. A shadow crossed the window that caused Reuben to look up and he saw three men standing back from the hitchrail and looking at their animals. He frowned, thinking there was something familiar about the three, and when one turned around as if looking for whoever had the pack mules, Reuben recognized the one known as Stink. Reuben turned slightly, and spoke low to Elly, "Don't look at the window, but we have company. Remember the three we ran into in Latham?"

Elly started to turn to the window to look out, but Reuben stopped her. "Don't turn!

They're standin' by the horses and lookin' at our packs. Looks like trouble to me."

"What're we gonna do?" asked Elly, absently touching the butt of her pistol holstered at her hip but under her jacket.

"Dunno. When we saw 'em before, we were on the stage, so they wouldn't know the horses, but they're mighty curious about the pack mules, or just the packs.

Guess we'll hafta just wait 'n' see. Maybe if we take our time, they might just leave."

Elly shook her head. "I'm guessing they're waiting for whoever owns the horses and mules to come out of this restaurant, and that would be us!"

"Ummhmm. But let's at least finish our breakfast."

26 /CONFRONTATION

T hey had a leisurely cup of coffee to top off their breakfast and did their best to ignore the three men that appeared to be waiting outside. But when Reuben saw some activity across the street in front of the stage station, he nodded to Elly. "Looks like they're openin' up at the station, and it appears those three hooligans are gone," as he looked out the window at the empty boardwalk in front of the restaurant.

Reuben settled their bill and ushered Elly to the door. She stepped out on the boardwalk, Reuben close behind, and just as they neared the hitchrail, the morning stage pulled around the buildings to rein up in front of the station, catching their attention. Elly turned to look at Reuben just as a man stepped behind him and grabbed his arms, jerking him back from the hitchrail. As she started to reach for Reuben, another man grabbed her from behind, wrapping his arms around her ribs and pinning her arms to her side. She started to shout an alarm, but a gruff voice growled, "Keep your mouth shut, missy, and you might live!"

Reuben was struggling with his captor, the man

called Stink who lived down to his moniker, the stench of his unwashed body adding to the calamity. Reuben fought against the man's iron grip, doing the unexpected by pushing back against him. They staggered across the boardwalk, slamming against the side of the building and Reuben dropped his chin to his chest and snapped his head back to smash against Stink's nose, splattering it across his face and loosening his grip. Stink shouted, "Yeeow!" as he tried to wrestle Reuben down. Reuben kicked out his feet, dropping all his weight on the weak grip of the man, bringing them both to the boardwalk. Reuben squirmed around and started to rise just as the attacker connected with a roundhouse swing that almost took his head off.

He went down on one shoulder but rolled away and came to his feet just as the attacker started to rise. Reuben brought his knee up under the man's chin, snapping his head back to slam against the side of the building. The attacker was stunned, and Reuben grabbed his shirt collar, jerked him to his feet and smashed his fist into the man's face, crushing his mouth and jaw, and slamming his head back. But Stink was angered and growled through the bloody maw that was his face and spread his arms wide as he charged his prey. Reuben dropped into a crouch as Stink charged, slapped Stink's hand aside as he twisted to the side, clasped his hands together and brought them both down on Stink's neck as he passed, dropping him face first onto the boardwalk. Stink growled and rolled away, coming to his feet, and showing an unexpected agility for such a big man. He snarled again, "I'm gonna tear you limb from limb, you cowardly snake! Stand still and fight like a man."

Reuben chuckled and held his open hands to the side. "What's the matter, Stink, you seem to be havin' a hard time! Not used to facin' a man that's not afraid of you? Can't handle a man by yourself and you hafta have help?"

Stink growled and charged again and as Reuben tried to twist aside, Stink stretched out his big arm and grabbed a handful of linen shirt, ripping and tearing as he clawed at Reuben's chest. He jerked Reuben close and brought up a left hook into his ribs, taking the wind from the smaller man. Reuben winced with pain, feeling the stab of a broken rib, but he dared not show his opponent he had scored a disabling blow and he twisted around, tearing himself from Stink's grip. They faced one another, both men gasping for air.

Reuben widened his stance, feinted to the left, and brought his right fist from the ground to bury it in Stink's gut, following it with a series of blows that hammered at the man's middle. Reuben felt the ribs give way and knew he had broken several of Stink's ribs, and blood and foam came from the man's mouth, dribbling onto his whiskers. Reuben knew the big man was hurt, but he didn't give way. Reuben stepped back, gasping for air and Stink threw a right jab just as Reuben turned, to make it a glancing blow, but he staggered, prompting Stink to drive in with another jab and a left cross that snapped Reuben's head to the side. Reuben saw the edge of the boardwalk and pushed away, lowering his shoulder to drive into the Stink's middle. He grabbed the big man's legs, lifted him and drove him into the big window of the restaurant, shattering the glass and dropping the big man on his back on the very table where he and Elly had just had their breakfast.

Both Elly and her captor had stepped off the boardwalk as she reached for the hitchrail, and they were now pushing against the rough rail. With her arms pinned at the elbows, she fought to use her hands and scratched at the arms of the man eliciting another warning, "Quit that, you little witch weasel, or I'll break your scrawny neck! And quit squirmin'!!"

Reuben turned to see the man, the one known as Baldy, holding Elly in a bearhug, but Elly had squirmed and twisted and reached into her jacket, dragging her pocket pistol free from the holster, and cocked it as she brought it down to her side. She dropped her head to see the booted feet of the man straddling hers and she pulled the trigger. The pistol blasted, the man screamed and released Elly. "You shot me!" he shouted, dancing on one foot, lifting the other as he fell to the edge of the board-walk. He saw the blood coming from the hole in his boot, pulled his foot up and whimpered, "My foot! You shot my foot! Ahhhheee!"

Reuben grinned as Elly cocked her pistol, stepping away from the man and holding the muzzle toward the attacker. She glanced toward Reuben and shouted, "Behind you!" Reuben twisted, dropping to one knee, and saw the big man Stink rising from the table, pistol in hand as he was bringing it to bear on Reuben, but Reuben grabbed for his pistol, felt an empty holster, and snatched his Bowie knife from the scabbard and in one fluid motion stretched out his arm, releasing the big razor-sharp knife to whisper through the air and bury itself in the chest of Stink. The big man's eyes flared as he saw the handle of the Bowie protruding from his chest, the haft of the blade flush against his dirty shirt where blood was soaking his chest and clothes. He looked up at Reuben, tried to lift his pistol and lost his grip, the weapon rattling to the floor, smashing more of the glass.

Reuben pulled the knife from Stink's chest, wiped it on the man's britches and slipped it into the scabbard.

He looked around, saw his pistol and holstered it then turned to look at Elly, and shouted, "The mules!"

In the middle of the street, the one known as Crocket was struggling with the mules. His manner with animals was to force them to his will and he had snatched the lead ropes of the mules, climbed aboard his horse, and tried to force the mules around to follow. But it has often been said, *If a mule don't wanna go, he ain't goin'!* As Crocket dug heels to his mount, dallied the two lead ropes around his saddle horn, the mules had reluctantly turned away from the hitchrail, but didn't like being jerked about. When Crocket hit the end of the lead ropes, both mules dropped anchor, dug in their heels and the taut lead ropes jerked the saddle up, digging the girth into the belly of the horse, and the fight was on. The lead ropes dug into the thigh of Crocket, pinning him into the saddle, but the horse was fighting to get away from the torturous Mexican rowel spurs that cut into his ribs and started bucking. He climbed the stairway of clouds and twisted, bent in half, and drove his front feet into the ground as if digging a grave for his rider. Crocket starting yelling and shouting curses as the girth tore loose from the saddle, the lead ropes of the mules dragging the saddle with the pinned Crocket still aboard. The horse, now free of his rider and saddle, continued his bucking, twisting in the middle, snorting his anger, and kicking at the slow-rising sun, as he cleared the street to make his exit from the civilization he had grown to hate. The mules decided they had enough of this mistreatment and started bucking and braying as they careened down the street, dragging Crocket and the saddle behind. Crocket tried to free himself from the entanglement of the broken latigo, the lead ropes of the mules that were dallied around the horn, the fenders and stirrups of the saddle and his own chaps, spurs and loose boots, all to no avail. The saddle twisted, putting Crocket on the underside, and being dragged on his back, ripping his jacket and shirt to allow the gravelly and rutted road to peel the hide from his back. He screamed and kicked, twisting in pain as a big rut in the road tipped the saddle, sending saddle and rider into the air to come crashing down on Crocket's shoulder, and tearing everything on his shoulder, shirt, jacket, hide and muscle. He was a bloody and screaming mess of flesh, bone and muscle.

Reuben looked at Elly. "C'mon, we gotta get 'em!" and leaped aboard the steel dust, as Elly stepped aboard the sorrel. Both gave chase, rode past the bouncing saddle, and caught up with the mules as they neared the edge of town, reined alongside, and reached down to grab the leads and halters, talking to try to settle them down. The familiar voices did the trick and within a short distance, they had the animals stopped. Reuben looked back at Crocket who was dirty, bloody, and battered, but still alive. He walked back and removed the leads from the saddle horn, looked at the bleeding Crocket, shook his head, and let him lie.

As he walked back to his steel dust, he stroked the neck of the mule, speaking softly and calmly to reassure the animal, "Easy boy. You done good, yessir, you did," and chuckled as he looked at Elly, still aboard her sorrel but holding tight to the lead of the other mule. She looked at Reuben, who looked at best somewhat bedraggled with rags of his shirt and jacket dangling like some remnant of a storm. "Aren't you gonna do something with him?" nodding toward Crocket, who still lay in the dirt, tangled with the saddle.

"Nope. You don't think he'd help me if that was me layin' there, do you?"

"Well, no, but you're not him."

"Thank Heaven," mumbled Reuben as he stepped aboard the steel dust. He reined his mount around and started back to town, Elly following close behind shaking her head. She looked down at Crocket as they passed, winced at the sight of his injuries, which were many as he appeared to be one bloody mass with little or no skin, and looked at her man who held his head high.

Several people had gathered on the street and boardwalk, watching the two assailants that lay on the boardwalk, one with a bloody chest and not breathing, the other whining and holding his foot. Reuben called out to a group that watched them ride down the street, "You got a doctor in this town?"

"Nope, but the barber doubles as a horse doctor and patch-em-up kinda doc."

"Tell him there's another'n back yonder, layin' in the middle of the road."

"The one what tried to steal your mules?"

"That's the one."

"You want the doc to look at that'n too?" pointing to the two on the boardwalk.

"If he wants, makes no difference to me," answered Reuben, nudging his gelding toward the stage station. He reined up at the rail, saw the stage loading luggage and mail, and with a nod to Elly, stepped down and tethered the animals.

"I heard you ask about a doctor, so you do care after all," she said, smiling up at Reuben.

"It's not that I care about them, they would have just as soon stolen everythin' and left us for dead and nobody in this town made a move to stop them, but, well, you know..." He shrugged, grinning.

"Yeah, I know. It's the right thing to do."

They pushed their way into the station, saw several people waiting to board the coach as soon as the hostlers and helpers finished loading the mail and packages, nodded to the station keeper and telegrapher, then asked, "Holladay here?"

The station keeper pointed to the door to the back office and turned his attention back to two men waiting at the counter, anxious to get tickets on the stage. Reuben and Elly pushed open the divider and rapped on the door, pushing it open at the invitation of someone inside. When they stepped through the door, Ben Holladay stood, stretched out his hand and with a broad smile, "Reuben, Elly, boy, you two are a sight for sore eyes! It is good to see you alive and well, we were beginning to wonder, no word and with the stage and freighters attacked. So, have a seat!" he motioned to the two chairs that sat opposite his desk. As he seated himself, he added, "I was just making plans to head to California, check on some stations, new routes, and such, but there's a little matter of a missing gold shipment."

Reuben grinned, glanced at Elly who was looking at him with a smirk, and looked back at Holladay, "Tain't missin', it's right outside on our packmules!"

"You brought it on pack mules?" asked Holladay, incredulous.

Reuben just nodded his head, then added, "And it sure is heavy. After you get that stage gone, maybe you could get somebody to bring it in for you."

"Get somebody? I'm so glad to hear you've got it; I'll carry it in myself! Come on, let's fetch it!" he demanded, making his way around the desk. He paused, looking at Reuben. "Say, were those your mules that those two tried to get away with just a little bit ago?"

"The same."

Holladay shook his head, and started for the door, mumbling something about a close call or other, as Reuben followed, grinning. Elly also followed but had no intention of helping pack in the heavy gold bars, that was something a lady left for the gentlemen to handle.

The heavy bars were in the bottom of the panniers, about fifty pounds per pannier, covered with trade blankets and light weight trinkets and gewgaws to make it appear there was nothing but trade goods for the Indians. They lifted off each of the panniers and carried them inside to deposit them in front of Holladay's desk. When they brought in the last one, a winded Holladay who was not used to much labor, sat in his chair, and motioned with his chin toward the panniers and looked at Reuben. "Show me!" he stated, grinning.

Reuben emptied each pannier, stacking the trade goods on the floor by the wall, and setting each gold bar on Holladay's desk. When he finished, there was two hundred pounds of gold bars covering the desk of the grinning owner of the stage line who stood, reached out to touch the bars, grinning ear to ear and looking at Reuben and Elly who sat back in their chairs, relieved to be rid of burdensome bars.

"You don't know how glad I am to see that," stated Holladay, nodding to the stack of bars. "I didn't know if the raiding rebels had gotten the gold and none of the bullwhackers, troopers, jehus, or shotgunners could tell me any different! And if they had gotten it, it might have put me outta business! So, you not only saved the Union and the stage line, but you also saved me from ruin!" He reached across the desk to shake Reuben's hand in appreciation.

Reuben stood to grasp the man's hand, grinning as he did. "Well, while the freighters and teamsters and troopers were fightin' the Rebels, we had to fight off outlaws and renegades, and we are just as happy to be rid of that as you are to get it!"

Holladay nodded, grinning, and sat back in his chair. He drew open his lap drawer, withdrew his checkbook and began writing. As he did, he explained, "This is not near what you deserve, but it will show my appreciation for what you have done!" He handed the check to Reuben and began, "Now, there's something else that I'd like you to look into..." but Reuben's upheld hand and frown stopped him. "What is it?"

"Mr. Holladay, although workin' for you has its rewards, and I appreciate what you've done," he lifted the check to emphasize the reward, "my little woman and I haven't had much time to ourselves. We plan on goin' west, maybe explore the mountains and such, but we need to spend some time alone, and that means away from outlaws, rebels, highwaymen, and anyone else that wants to interfere with our lives."

Holladay grinned, nodding. "I understand. And I don't blame you at all. But since you're going west, there might be some other opportunities. So, maybe you could stop into one of our stations every now and then and see if there might be a telegram for you."

Reuben grinned, stood, and reached in his pocket and withdrew the marshal's badge. He lay it on the desk as Elly did the same, then looked up at Holladay. "And as for these, if you would return them to the marshal, I would appreciate it."

Holladay grew somber, slowly shaking his head. "I'm afraid I have no authority to do that. You took an oath, so, you might want to hold onto those. I will pass the word along at the first opportunity, and there will be a telegram waiting for you with instructions about what to do with those, but in the meantime, well, you just never know."

Reuben picked up the badges, handed one to Elly and put the other in his pocket. "As far as I'm concerned, we are about as 'unofficial' as we can be, but we will look for that telegram, however, not any too soon."

"I understand. What with the war that may be winding down, and the gold rush also falling off, maybe the new governor will see his way clear to appoint another marshal and will have no need of you two."

"Right now, we need to load up the mules and get to the livery. We have a couple horses there we are anxious to get, then we'll be puttin' some distance between us and this place!"

Holladay stood again, offered his hand. "Thanks again. I will always be in your debt so if there's ever anything I can do for you, just ask."

With handshakes all around, Reuben and Elly packed up the panniers and soon had them back on the mules. They swung aboard and started for the livery where they left the Blue Roan and the Leopard Appaloosa, and both were anxious to see their old friends.

They stepped into the shade of the big livery barn, Reuben gave out his usual whistle and a head came up and whinnied from a stall toward the back. Reuben recognized the Blue Roan that had been his partner and friend for some time, and he quickened his step, Elly coming behind him carrying the black fur ball she was calling Buster. Blue whinnied again, getting a little fidgety in the stall as Reuben lowered the bar at the rear and stepped alongside the roan. He ran his hand along the spine of the big horse, scratching as he went, and reaching for the roan's neck, he talked with him, "Hey, Blue, how ya' doin' boy? You are lookin' good, my friend." The big gelding bent around and reached for his friend with probing lips as Reuben stroked the side of his head, behind his ears and down his forehead. The two friends were savoring the reunion as Elly spotted her leopard appaloosa who had lifted her head over the rails at the ruckus. She whinnied as she spotted Elly and received a greeting, "Hey girl! How you doing?" Elly put the pup down to roam at will while she came alongside her mare, stroking and talking all the while.

They backed the horses out of the stalls as the liveryman came alongside. "Howdy, folks! Good to see you back! I was kinda gettin' attached to these hyar horses and was hopin' you'd ferget to come back! Even had a few folks askin' if'n they was fer sale, but I had ta' put 'em off since I figgered you'd be comin' back."

"Well, we've got a couple other horses and a pair o' mules we might make a deal on," countered Reuben.

"You mean those two you rode in on?"

"Ummhmm, and the mules."

"Wal, I can always use the mules, what with the stage line an' such, but I got too many horses already. I got some out yonder in the corral that should be in these stalls, and will be, soon's you take your horses."

Reuben glanced at Elly, gave a short nod, then turned to the liveryman. "You got my mule handy?"

"Shore do, I'll fetch him for you. But you just said you was wantin' to sell two, so, what'cha gonna do?"

"I'll sell you those two," nodding to the two that were tethered outside the livery, "and one of the packs and such. But I'll keep the one we left with you; he and this roan are kinda buddies and I'd hate to separate 'em."

"What about the other gear you left in my tack room?"

"I'll sort through it; we can dicker on what I don't need."

"Alrighty then, I'll fetch yore mule!" replied the man, walking away toward the corral. He snatched a halter from a peg on a post and disappeared around the corner. Reuben looked to Elly. "Looks like we're takin' the other horses to the ranch!"

"I'm glad. They're good horses and I'd hate to see 'em end up in the hands of someone like that thug we just tangled with."

AFTER ALL THE DICKERING AND TRADING, REUBEN AND Elly kept their new saddles and other gear, traded the old tack and two mules to the liveryman, and even after boarding their animals for most of three weeks, he ended up owing them money when all was said and done. They took a meal at the restaurant and used the money from the liveryman to pay for the broken window and their meal and mounted up just after midday to start their return journey to the Slade ranch.

"We'll go as far as we can 'fore dark and make camp so we don't ride into the ranch in the middle of the night. The Cash brothers might mistake us for a raiding party or outlaws and start shootin' 'fore they know who we are!"

Elly chuckled at the thought. "That's alright. There's plenty of good campsites along the river and we can enjoy the stars." She lifted her eyes to the empty sky. "No clouds, and the moon is prob'ly only a quarter, so it'll be a pretty night."

"As long as we don't get woke up by a raidin' party, outlaws, or mama bears!"

"Oh, you're a bundle of good thoughts!" she answered, giggling. She rode beside Reuben, looking over at him and smiled, thinking how good it was to have nothing else to think about than their time together. With her fingers stroking the thick fur of Buster, she let a memory intrude on her blissful thoughts. "What're we gonna do about the young'uns?"

"Dunno. We sent that telegram to their uncle but didn't get an answer. Maybe we'll stay on this side of the river, stop at Spring Hill, see if they can check with Julesburg and find if there's been an answer. We should be there 'fore dark and will still have time to cross over and make camp."

"What if the uncle doesn't answer, or doesn't want 'em?" asked Elly, voicing the question both had harbored but didn't want to voice.

Reuben just shook his head, looking toward the river with glassy eyes, his mind wandering and wondering. They had both grown close to the little ones, but what would they do with two children along on their travels? They weren't ready to settle down and make a home, although they planned to someday, but right now they did not have any inclination as to where or when.

Elly also was quiet and introspective, considering the children. She loved Mary and her heart stirred at the remembrance of the little girl cuddling up to her when they rode together and when they slept. She smiled at the image of the two together. She wanted children of her own and had often talked with her sister and mother about having a large family one day, but they did not even have a home of their own, much less one for children. She shook her head and wiped the tears from her eyes, turning away so Reuben would not see them.

They were riding into the setting sun; the scattered clouds were showing golden bellies, and long lances of gold and orange pierced the clouds and disappeared in the heavens. The west facing trees had a glow as shadows stretched long to the east. Reuben frowned, looking to the north side of the river at a rising wisp of dust, and nudged Blue to the edge of the river where gnarly cottonwoods lifted their barren grey trunks like skeletal fingers of long dead trees. Reuben was trailing both spare horses and Elly trailed the pack mule as they pushed into a clearing at the riverbank. Reuben stood in his stirrups, shading his eyes against the glare of the lowering sun, and grinned as he turned to Elly. "Looks like an entire native village movin' south. They'll prob'ly make camp 'fore crossin' the river and unless I miss my guess, they're friends of ours."

"Friends?" frowned Elly, also standing in her stirrups for a better look but she couldn't make out anything but a dust cloud. She looked at Reuben, waiting for an answer, and at his broad grin, she guessed, "You mean Little Raven and the Arapaho?"

"Reckon so, but we'll wait till they make camp," he explained as he looked around the little clearing where they stood. "This'll do for us, little shade yonder, grass for the animals, plenty of firewood. What say?"

Elly had also given the site a once-over and nodded as she swung a leg over the rump of the Appaloosa to step to the ground. They quickly made camp, tethered the extra horses and mule, and mounted up to cross the river and visit their friends. Elly was more anxious to see Running Antelope and Wind in Her Hair than she realized and could not help smiling at the anticipated reunion. Reuben looked back at her, grinned, and said, "I don't think you smile that much when you're waitin' for me to return."

"That's cuz we're never apart! Besides, they did a lot for us and they're the first friends I've had among the natives. They're special people!"

"They are that, and it'll be good to visit with Little Raven, but I'm wonderin' why they're travelin' south. I thought they were makin' their summer encampment up north, closer to the better buffalo country."

"I reckon we'll find out soon enough," answered Elly, nodding toward four riders coming their way. The warriors were the protectors of the people and did not recognize the two riders approaching their camp. They were armed with rifles and lances, and the leader of the four lifted his lance that had two scalp locks dangling, and shouted at the intruders in English, "Do not come! Who are you and why are you here?"

"We are friends of Little Raven and Red Bear, I am Reuben, and this is Yellow Bird, we have come to visit with our friends."

The warriors looked from one to the other, back to Reuben, then motioned for them to follow.

"The white man chief, Evans, came to our camp and said we must return to the land to the south. The land by the old Bent's Fort, they now call Fort Wise. Evans said he heard we were planning a war against the whites and that his soldiers would come against us and kill many to stop the war," explained Little Raven, chief of the *Hinono' eino*, the Southern Arapaho people. Little Raven was an impressive figure, broad shouldered, leathered face, his greying hair hung in long braids over his shoulders, partially obscuring the eagle feather shoulder piece he wore over his beaded buckskin tunic. Three notched eagle feathers adorned the top knot at the back of his head, and he carried himself regally. Known as the great peacemaker, he had been a part of the entourage that signed the Fort Wise treaty that forbid passage of white men across their lands and promised annuities of thirty thousand dollars per year to the tribe, promises the government failed to fulfill.

"Were you? Were you plannin' a war?" asked Reuben.

"I went to your great leader in Washington, Lincoln, and he gave me this," holding a medal that hung from a ribbon around his neck, "and this," holding a letter from President Lincoln, "that says I make peace with the White man. But we cannot eat medals and letters!" tossing the letter aside. "Our brothers, the *Tsétsêhéstâhese*, Cheyenne, say we are not bound by the treaty because the white man has not honored it. They want to take back the land they say we gave to the white man," he waved his arms wide to indicate the land where they were. "The Dog Soldiers say our chiefs did not understand what we signed, and we should take back the land."

"Are you goin' to war?"

"We are going back to the land by the river *Napeste*, what the whites call Arkansas, where the Fort Wise stands. They say we must be there to keep the soldiers, the big soldier man named Chivington that talks war with natives, from coming against us. We will be at peace with the white man as we have always been."

As they spoke, Red Bear, Little Raven's first wife brought platters of food for the men while Elly, or Yellow Bird, and Running Antelope and Wind in Her Hair sat around the fire inside the tipi and talked about the men and their lives. "Have you found life with Reuben to be what you wanted?" asked Wind, smiling at Elly, and putting her hand to her mouth to muffle her giggles.

"It has been exciting! And wonderful, and I am happy to be his woman," answered Elly, smiling.

Running Antelope leaned toward her, nodding to her belly. "Will you soon have children?"

"We are not in a hurry, but we rescued two children, a boy and girl, from some renegades and they have no home, so..." she shrugged as she dropped her eyes thinking about the youngsters.

"Where are the little ones now?" asked Red Bear.

"We go to them tomorrow. We left them with some friends that have a ranch not far from here."

The women looked to one another, smiling, and knowing the pull felt by a woman when she has little ones that look to her for protection and life. The three women before her had a total of eleven children, with Red Bear's first born only twelve summers and all the children already put down for the night in the lodges of the women. Four were snuggled together under buffalo robes at the back of the lodge where they sat, and Red Bear looked to them as they talked of family.

Little Raven had been joined by chief Shave-Head, another of the Arapaho chiefs that had joined the meeting with Governor Evans and was also taking his people south to Fort Wise. "Have you seen any of the Dog Soldiers in your travels?" asked Shave-Head, looking askance to Reuben.

"I did a little tradin' with Lean Bear after our time with Little Raven."

"You traded with Lean Bear? After the signing of the treaty at Fort Wise, he was angry with the whites and swore he would kill every white man he met. How is it that you could trade with him?"

"He had somethin' I wanted, and I had somethin' he wanted. He had two white women captives. He and his warriors had attacked a ranch not far from here and taken the women captive. I had a 'far-shootin'' rifle that he wanted, and he also knew there was a rifle trained on him from the trees, so we traded," Reuben chuckled as he told the story. "'Course, he didn't know it was my new wife that had the rifle!"

The two chiefs looked at one another and started laughing to know that a woman had fooled the great Lean Bear into a trade with a white man. "That story will be told around the fires for many times to come!" declared Shave-Head, laughing again.

The visit continued into the night until the women came from the lodge, encouraging the men to break it up for the night as Elly stretched and yawned to give Reuben the sign that she was tired. Shave-Head looked at her, then to Reuben and motioned with his eyes and hand to ask if she was the one that buffaloed Lean Bear, and with a broad grin, Reuben nodded, making Shave-Head start laughing again.

THE GREY LINE OF EARLY MORNING STRETCHED ACROSS the eastern horizon as Reuben came from the little butte behind their camp. Since his time in the war and after his heartfelt renewal in his Christian life, Reuben had tried to establish a habit of greeting each new day in the presence of his Lord with time in prayer, and would usually find a lone promontory for that solitude. Returning to camp, a glance to his left showed the people of a wagon train that apparently moved in while they were visiting the Arapaho, rousing around to break camp and get back on the trail. He guessed there to be about a dozen to fifteen wagons, big enough to be well manned and armed, but small enough to be a target for a war party of Cheyenne Dog Soldiers. *Maybe I better go let them know about the Arapaho. I'd hate to see some trigger-happy settlers start a war.* He walked into camp where Elly was playing with the pup as she waited for the coffee to boil. He smiled at the sight and said, "I just spotted a wagon train back a ways, thought I better warn them about the Arapaho." He walked to the Roan and started saddling the gelding as he looked back over his shoulder. "Look to be settlers instead of gold hunters, but greenhorns get a little scared at the sight of a big bunch of natives and start shootin'. Don't want that!"

"No, we don't. But you mind your manners too, most folks don't like strangers riding in and telling 'em what to do. I'll have breakfast ready when you get back!" she declared, picking up the pup and stroking him behind the ears. "You think we'll make the ranch by noon?"

"Well, we wanna stop at Spring Hill and check on a telegram, then it's just a short ride past there, across the river and such, so yeah, prob'ly."

"Good. I'm excited about seeing the kids!" she smiled coyly to make Reuben wonder what she was up to, but he knew better than ask. He stepped aboard the roan and swung around to get to the wagons before they started on the trail. As he approached the camp, he hailed the nearest wagon, "Hello the camp! Alright if I come in?"

A storekeeper looking type stepped from behind his wagon, thumbs in his galluses as he looked at the stranger, nodded, "If you're peaceable, come on in! Coffee's on and welcome!"

Reuben grinned, nudging his roan between the wagons, and swung down to stretch out his hand to shake with the man. "Mornin', I'm Reuben Grundy!"

"Mornin', I'm Eustis Hackmeyer, and this here's my wife, Hortense, and my son, Eben," he pointed to a boy of about ten that stood partially hidden behind his father's leg and his woman that was busy stirring a pan full of breakfast that Reuben couldn't identify.

"Pleased to meet you, ma'am, Eben." He lifted his eyes to Eustis. "Who's your wagon master?"

"Don't have one. We been kinda sharin' the duties since our wagon master was kilt when some Injuns attacked us several days back. Lost him, the scout, couple others. But we did alright against 'em. Now we figger to go into Colorado territory, maybe Denver City, find us a place an' settle down."

"Lookin' for gold, are ya?" asked Reuben.

"Nah, farmland mostly. We come from Missouri, gettin' away from them bushwhackers and the rest of the war. Several of our men did their share of fightin', and now we want to get our families away from all that."

"I understand. I did my time as well. So, are you the man to talk to about the safety of the wagons?"

"What'chu mean, the safety of the wagons?"

"Are you?"

"Well, the one what's been doin' more of the leadin' is Hector Mitchum. He's around here somewhere."

"Does the boy know who he is?"

Eustis looked back at his son. "Eben, you run fetch Hector. Tell him there's a man here needs to talk to him, real important! Now run!"

The boy glanced at Reuben, stuck his thumb in his mouth and ran off down the line of wagons in search of the replacement wagon master. Within moments, a lanky man that stood well over six feet but skinny as a rail, strode into the circle of the Hackmeyer family. "Who's so important to drag me up here this early?" he demanded with a deep voice that contrasted with his gangly appearance.

Reuben stood, extended his hand, and introduced himself, "I'm Reuben Grundy. I just rode over to give you folks a bit of a warnin' about some Indians."

"Indians! Where?" he asked, looking beyond the wagon circle expecting to see a horde of attackers charging the train.

Reuben grinned. "No, it's not what you think. Although you are in Indian country, as far as I know you're in no danger."

"Oh, but I thought..." he frowned as he looked at the stranger standing before him.

"Let me explain. This country was the land of the Arapaho and the Cheyenne until it was recently taken from them by a treaty signed at Fort Wise. But most of the natives didn't agree with the terms and some are wantin' to take it back. That would be the Cheyenne Dog Soldiers. But the Arapaho are peaceful, always have been, and they are just up there," nodding behind him toward the upstream area, "and will be crossin' your trail shortly after full sun-up. And like I said, they're peaceful and not lookin' for a fight. And since Eustis here said you folks had a bit of a fight with natives recently, I thought you might want to know you're not in danger."

"Not in danger?! If there's Injuns, we're in danger. We need to kill ever one o' them heathens 'fore they kill more of us!" shouted a man that had walked up to the circle while Reuben was talking. He was a scruffy looking, but solidly built man outfitted in typical farmer attire with linsey Woolsey shirt, corded britches, tall boots and galluses all under a bearded face and a floppy hat. His black eyes glared from under the hat, and his snarl parted his whiskers. Hector, the wagon master, turned to face the intruder and calmly spoke, "Now, Mitchell, we need to hear the man out. If we can avoid a fight, we need to; there's too many women and kids among us to risk another fight!"

Hector turned back to Reuben. "You need to understand, Mitchell lost his wife and son in the fight we were in last week, this side of Kearny."

"I allus knew them heathens couldn't be trusted. Ever one of 'em needs to take a dirt bath!" declared Mitchell.

Reuben stood to face the man. "If you try to go against this bunch, every one of you will probably be

209

killed. As I told Hector here, these are peaceful Arapaho and have always been friendly with white men. But they will defend their women and children, just like you. The difference is, they have about a hundred fifty to two hundred battle proven warriors, all well-armed and you wouldn't stand a chance!" stated Reuben, emphatically. He turned back to Hector, "They're crossin' the river, headin' south, goin' down to Fort Wise by the Arkansas river. It might be wise for you to just take a day of rest here and they'll be long gone by the time you pass Spring Hill stage station."

Hector looked from Eustis to Mitchell, back to Reuben. He extended his hand and said, "I thank you for the warning, and I reckon that would be the safest way to avoid a fight. I think most of our folks would enjoy a day of rest anyway. Thank you."

Mitchell turned on his heel and stomped away, mumbling about the need to kill the heathen Indians and Reuben knew there was still a very real chance for trouble, even if it came from just one man. He shook hands with Eustis, nodded to Hortense, and stepped back aboard Blue. He looked at the family and said, "Good meetin' you folks. Now you have a safe journey, and may you find that farmland you're lookin' for, there's a lot of it between here and Denver City." He tipped his hat to the lady and reined the roan around to return to Elly and his waiting breakfast.

T he smell of bacon frying welcomed Reuben back into camp, but the smiling face of his bride brought him to a quick stop as he slid from his saddle to take her in his arms, but the black fur ball in her arms was crowded between them and a chuckling Reuben's attention was turned to the bacon. "Eggs? Where'd you get eggs?"

"Oh, there were a couple ducks at the edge of the water that couldn't quit bragging and quacking, so I thought they wanted to share their bounty, so, there ya' go!" answered a grinning Elly, as she put the pup down and stirred the scrambled eggs in the skillet. "The coffee's ready if you wanna pour yourself a cup. This is 'bout ready and I'll dish it up." She looked up at Reuben, "I take it your mission was successful?"

"Yeah," he drawled, "but..."

"But what?"

"There always seems to be a troublemaker in the crowd. Can't say as I blame him, though. They had a run-in with some Pawnee, and he lost his wife and son, so he's decided all Indians are heathens and killers and need to pay for killin' his family."

"Was it just him, or were there others?"

"I think it was just him. They lost their wagon master and scout, prob'ly the only ones that knew anythin' about the native peoples, but the rest seemed to agree it would be best to wait a day and avoid the Arapaho. But that one fella, Mitchell was his name, might try somethin'."

"Well, let's have our breakfast and get on to Spring Hill station and see about the telegram," resolved a determined Elly.

Reuben glanced at her, suspected something was going on in her thinking and guessed it to be about the youngsters. He understood her emotional attachment to the little ones; he felt it too, but to take two youngsters into the wilderness of the mountains and the unsettled west might be more than they could handle. And would it be best for the little ones? He shook his head as he reached to accept the offered plate of eggs, bacon, sliced cat-tail shoots, and the steaming cup of coffee.

The Overland Trail road, used by the stage line and many settlers and gold seekers, lay between the South Platte River and some low-rising sandhills to the south. After breaking camp and riding from the bosque, Reuben led them onto the low hills for a promontory to watch the progress of the Arapaho village. They stepped down and found a seat to watch the passage of the village.

With almost a hundred lodges packed on travois trailed by horses led by the women, the crossing of the shallow waters at the wide bend of the river progressed as if there was no impediment. With sandbars, gravel bottom and slow current, it was no more than cool water on hot feet and refreshing even though it was early in the morning. The two villages, one led by Little Raven the other by Shave-Head, they numbered somewhere around three hundred people, plus the many horses, dogs, and the rambunctious children. Under other circumstances and with different people, it would be chaotic pandemonium, but these were people that were accustomed to moving entire villages within hours of the proclamation. Now they were bound for what they hoped would be their home for the rest of the summer and perhaps into the winter. They had taken ample supply of buffalo and were well prepared for the next few months, at least until the southern migration of the buffalo herds when they would have their fall hunt.

"Aren't they amazing?" asked Elly, watching the procession with wonder.

"Yes, they are, and to think this is their way of life, movin' two, three times a year. Followin' the buffalo, movin' with the seasons, seldom campin'in familiar ground, it's nothin' like our people that want to have deep roots, a home for a lifetime and more," replied Reuben, his thoughts wandering from his past and family home to the prospects and hopes of the future.

"Do you think we'll have those deep roots soon or do you think our home will still be on the backs of our horses?"

Reuben was silent as he thought of her question, glanced at her as she watched the Arapaho, and knew part of her thinking was including the youngsters. But he wondered about what the children's family would say when they got the telegram; they naturally belonged with family and should be there. But if they had to put them on the stage to Missouri, would Elly be able to give them up, even though it was family?

As he pondered the wishes of his wife, his focus was brought back to the present when she asked, "What is that? *Who* is that?" she was pointing to a rider coming from the east on the Overland trail, riding as if his life depended on it, slapping reins to the rump of his horse and with what appeared to be a rifle laying across his pommel. He was maybe two hundred yards away and his horse was in an all-out run.

Reuben jumped to his feet, shading his eyes from the rising sun. "That's Mitchell, the man from the wagons that wants to fight the Arapaho! We've got to stop him!" He tossed the leads for the spare horses to Elly, swung aboard the Roan and slapped legs to the big gelding to tear off down the slope, taking an angle to cut off the rider. The roan felt the urgency as Reuben lay along his neck, encouraging him, "C'mon boy, we've got to beat him!" as the roan's mane slapped in Reuben's face, his tail high and flagging, his neck stretched out, and his long legs stretching across the grassy flats.

Mitchell had grabbed his rifle and easily held it out, gripped as a pistol, and screamed as he charged the procession of Arapaho. He was still more than two hundred yards from the procession and Reuben could hear him as he shouted, "I'm gonna kill every one of you!" as he fired his first shot into the crowd, the big rifle boomed and bucked, spitting smoke, making the man grab at it with both hands. He dropped the reins over the neck of his mount and struggled to work the lever on the big Spencer. The Arapaho began to scatter, warriors charging toward the threat, women and children pushing away. Reuben lay low on the neck of the roan. "C'mon Blue, you can do it!" and the gelding seemed to quicken his pace, stretching out with longer strides, his sides heaving.

Reuben snatched his pistol from the holster at his hip, yet not wanting to kill the man. He fired a shot over his head to get his attention off the natives, but he would not be dissuaded. One handed, Mitchell lifted the rifle, trying to take sight on the scattering Arapaho, but the galloping gait of his big bay horse, the rutted road, and the fleeing targets made him grab the weapon with both hands, fearful of losing his grip. Reuben was nearing the man and fired another shot to turn him back, but Mitchell lifted his rifle to his shoulder, tucking the reins in the fold of his arm, determined to make his shot count. But the Remington bucked in Reuben's hand and the bullet buried itself in Mitchell's shoulder. The crazed man slumped, turned, and glared at the new threat and struggled to bring his rifle to bear on Reuben as he came closer.

Reuben dug heels into Blue's ribs and the horse lunged to drive his chest into the shoulder of Mitchell's mount, knocking him to the side. The big bay stumbled, his front legs giving way, and went down on his shoulder to tumble to the ground, throwing his rider into a big clump of sage. The impact brought a scream from the downed man who had lost his rifle and was fighting his way free from the tangled brush. Reuben reined up and swung around just as five warriors brought their mounts to a sliding stop beside the brush, two rifles trained on the man, and two warriors with lances, one with a drawn bow and arrow. When Mitchell freed himself from the brush, he looked around, wide-eyed, and spotted Reuben pushing through the circle of warriors.

"YOU! You're a white man and you're with these heathen? Get me outta here!"

"Why? You are right where you wanted to be, in the middle of these warriors! You wanted to kill them, remember? And you tried! So, why should I get you out of there?"

"You're a white man, and these are...are...heathen Injuns!"

"These are Arapaho people; this is their land. You are the intruder and are not welcome, especially not now. You could have killed or injured their women and children and they have every right to kill you, but look around. These 'heathen' as you call them have spared your life." As Mitchell looked around the circle, he saw all the warriors had lowered their weapons. "Now, get your horse and go back to the wagons before they change their mind!"

Mitchell looked around, saw his horse standing ground tied about twenty yards away, and with a quick glance to the warriors, started toward his mount. As he passed the sage, he spotted his rifle in the dirt, looked at it and took a glimpse back to Reuben and the warriors. He suddenly dropped to one knee to grab his weapon, and jacked a round and eared back the hammer as he came to his feet and turned, but was stopped when Reuben's pistol bucked and another round from the .44 blossomed at his chest as he tried to lift the rifle, but it slipped from his hands. He looked at the blood dripping onto his hands from the wound, back to Reuben, and fell to his knees and onto his face to lie still.

The warriors sat silent, looking from Reuben to the man by the sage, then reined their mounts around and rejoined their people. Reuben nudged Blue to the sage, then to the bay horse that stood, head high and ears forward, picked up the reins and led the horse close to the body. He stepped down, ground tied Blue and struggled to lift Mitchell's body to lay across his saddle. He cut the tie downs at the back of the saddle to use to secure the body and turned to mount up just as Elly rode up beside him. She looked at her man and knew what he was feeling, but also knew there was nothing she could say that would help. They reined around to take Mitchell's body back to the wagons and rode silently, side by side.

As they neared the wagons, a handful of people, led by the wagon master, Hector, walked from the circle. He spoke, "We're not surprised, we tried to stop him, but he wouldn't listen. There was nothing we could do."

"Well, I thought it best to bring him back. I figgered he'd have a wagon and goods to divide, maybe some of your folks could put things to good use. Or if you know if he has other family, to let them know."

"He had no one. After losing his wife and son, he was all alone. But we'll take care of the burying and we're beholden to you for what you've done."

Reuben nodded, handed the reins of the burdened mount to the fill-in wagon master and he and Elly turned and rode back toward the next stage station and the expected telegram.

T he Spring Hill station was built by the Central
Overland California and Pikes Peak Express
stagecoach line that was bought out by Ben Holladay and
was one of the better stations on the line. A home
station, it was also equipped with a telegraph and the
buildings afforded overnight accommodations and meals
for the travelers as well as a large barn, blacksmith shop,
and corrals for the animals. As was true with most of the
stations, they also offered most travelers the same
accommodations, with the coach passengers getting
priority.

When Reuben and Elly rode into the yard, they were
greeted by one of the hostlers who was coming from the
barn, leading two teams of mules. "Howdy, folks!
Welcome! Make yourself ta' home, stage comin' in and
the meal's ready!" As they started to step down, Reuben
turned at the distant sound of the messenger's bugle
warning of the arrival of the coach. He grinned, glanced
to Elly and they reined up at the hitchrail. He looked at
the hostler and asked, "Telegrapher in?"

"Yup! Right yonder!" he declared pointing to the smaller of the two log buildings.

Reuben looked at Elly. "If you wanna go get us a seat at the dinner table, I'll check on the telegram!"

Elly laughed, shaking her head. "Do you really think I'd let you get that telegram without me?" and followed him through the door.

A middle-aged balding man with a small visor riding his eyebrows looked up at the visitors and asked, "What can I do for you folks?"

Reuben stepped to the counter. "Do you have a telegram for a Reuben Grundy?"

The man frowned, nodded, and turned to his desk where the key sat amongst stacks of papers and other paraphernalia. The shelf behind the desk was lined with the batteries and wires necessary for the telegram and the man picked up a small stack of papers and started sorting through the sheath. He glanced up to Reuben. "Came in last night. Didn't make much sense to me but here ya go!" he stated as he handed the gram to Reuben.

Reuben turned his back to the counter and unfolded the paper, Elly pulling at his elbow so she could see as well. *Reuben Grundy, Overland Stage Line, Colorado. Cannot take children, lost my husband. My sister, Gretchen and husband want them. Please advise.* Elly looked up at Reuben and seemed to melt at his side, holding to his arm and dropping her eyes as she slowly turned back to the doorway. Reuben followed her outside and stopped by the hitchrail, looking at his woman leaning against the rail, downcast.

"I reckon we'll have to talk to Micah and Mary first, don'tchu think?" asked Reuben. "If this Gretchen and her husband are like their Uncle Henry, I don't reckon I'd be

219

for sendin' them back, but if they're good folks, the children belong with family."

"I know, it would be the right thing for them to be back with family and have a home of their own and a school and such, but..." she shrugged as she turned away.

"Then I reckon we need to get us a meal and start for the ranch and talk with the young'uns," suggested Reuben, touching Elly's elbow to steer her to the dining room. He knew she had been thinking about taking the children under wing and this was a disappointment, but there was nothing else he could do for her but give her time and let things work out the right way.

THE WOMEN WERE ENJOYING THE SHADE OF THE PORCH AS they worked at preparing things for the evening meal. The older women, Ethel and Gladys were snapping beans with the younger girl, Evangeline, helping. Sadie was working at a butter plunger, churning butter while Mabel was shucking the first picking of corn with the help of little Mary. As Reuben and Elly rode into the yard, Mary was the first to see them and called out, "Elly, Elly!" and stood to wave at the newcomers. Elly quickly swung down and spread her arms wide to welcome the little girl into her arms and give her a warm hug.

Reuben took the reins of Elly's Appy, pushed his roan toward the porch and asked, "Where's Micah?"

Sadie stood, hands on hips and walked to the edge of the porch, smiling. "Oh, he's out with the other men, moving some cattle. Couldn't get him off that horse and had to let him go with the men; wouldn't have it any other way. Said something 'bout not wanting to hang around a 'bunch o' wimmen,'" she explained, laughing.

She nodded to the other horses and asked, "Couldn't make up your mind which ones to ride?"

Reuben chuckled, glancing back at the spare horses. "Nah, couldn't sell 'em for a good price, thought you folks would appreciate some fresh mounts."

Ethel stood, and walked to the edge of the porch, shading her eyes from the midday sun and looked at the animals. "Aren't those the ones you rode in here on a couple days ago?"

"That's right. But this'n," leaning down to pat the neck of Blue, "and me have a connection and same way with that'n," nodding to the Appaloosa of Elly's, "and Elly. So, thought we'd just drop 'em off here in case we ever need a spare when we're passin' through."

Ethel smiled, nodding. "Well, put 'em all in the barn, fork 'em some hay, give 'em some grain and come on in the house to get outta this sun!" she declared, stepping back to her rocking chair. With a nod to Elly, Reuben took the animals to the barn to rub them down and give them some grain, knowing Elly would like some time with Mary and the womenfolk.

Reuben had just finished the rubdowns and feeding of the animals when he heard several horses riding up to the barn entrance. He walked from the stall beside Blue, saw the men outside, and walked out to meet them. He was greeted first by the Cash brothers who chimed almost in unison, "Reuben! Welcome back!" as they stepped down from their mounts.

A quick glance showed Micah aboard a dapple-grey gelding that was about fourteen hands and was easily handled by the youngster as he nudged him closer, "Hi, Reuben!" he greeted. "How'd you like my horse?" he asked, reaching down to stroke the gelding's neck, and smiling broadly.

"Looks like a mighty fine horse, and just your size too! So, you been out workin' cattle with the other men?"

"Ummhmmm. I like workin' cattle!" he declared. Jeremiah Cash came alongside and said, "Well, we're done for the day, so you need to get down and take the gear off, rub down your horse, and get him some water and grain. Think you can do that?"

"Done it before, just watch me!" he answered, looking at Reuben to be sure he was watching.

The boy swung his leg over the grey's rump and with both legs dangling, he belly-slid down the fender of the saddle to the ground, reins in hand and started for the barn. He grinned up at Reuben as he walked past. Reuben glanced at Jeremiah and was reassured when Jeremiah said, "I'll make sure he's alright, but he's provin' to be quite the cowboy!" and walked behind Micah into the barn to put the grey in a stall. Jeremiah called over his shoulder, "Go on in the house, we'll be right along!"

Reuben went to the water trough and pump, pumped the handle for some fresh water and doused his head and hands, felt for the slightly soiled towel, and wiped the water away. After a quick check to be sure his hands were clean, he ran his fingers through his hair and started for the house. The chatter from within bid him enter and as he stepped inside, Mary ran to him, wrapped her arms around his legs and looked up, "Hi, Reuben!" smiling broadly.

Reuben bent down to lift her up and set her on his hip, smiling at her and answered, "Well, hello, Mary! You been helpin' the ladies?"

"Ummhmm, I was he'pin' Mabel shuck corn!"

"You were? My, that's sumpin'!" he declared, getting a smile from the little one in return. She wiggled and he sat her down, stepping behind Elly who sat at the table, talking with the ladies. Sadie looked up at him and asked, "So, you decided what to do?" Reuben frowned, not certain about the question, until Sadie clarified, "About the children?"

"Nope. I thought we'd all talk it over, us," motioning to Elly and the other ladies, "and the young'uns. I figger they got a say in this, don't you?"

"Ummmhmm, and I'm glad you included us," motioning to the women at the table, "in that 'talking over'," answered Sadie.

223

S ometimes things are more easily discussed over a good meal. Many of the world's problems would be lessened, wars shortened, and families healed, if folks would just sit together and enjoy a good meal. It's not easy to get upset when a piece of fresh hot apple pie is set before you by a smiling and cheerful woman. And it is doubly so when children are involved, for what growing boy cannot be easily convinced of just about anything when his stomach is full of good food?

An extra table was butted up to the one in the large dining room of the Slade ranch house, extra chairs were brought in, and everyone was seated around a table laden with sumptuous looking and delectable smelling foodstuffs. As everyone joined hands, Mabel's father, Elbert, the long-time ramrod of the Slade ranch, led the combined families in a prayer of thanksgiving for the feast, family, and friends, and the impromptu festivities were under way.

When the pie tins were scraped clean, the table cleared, and fresh coffee poured, Reuben looked at Micah who sat beside Jeremiah Cash and asked, "Do you remember some family named Matthew and Gretchen Wilkins?"

"Ummhmm, we called 'em Uncle Matt and Aunt Gretchen, but they wasn't really related. Momma said they was cousins or sumpin'."

"Are they nice folks?" asked Reuben, glancing from Micah to Mary and back.

"Ummhmmm. Aunt Gretchen always had candy for us, and Uncle Matt would give us both a penny. They have a big store in town and always had big jars of candy on the counter. I like the horehound best!" declared Micah, glancing to a nodding Mary.

"Well, Micah, Mary," began Reuben, looking at the two youngsters that were seated between the Cash brothers, looking a little fragile and fearful, "we need to decide where you two should live. Your Uncle Henry and Aunt Margaret, back in Missouri on the farm, can't take you, but her sister, Gretchen and her husband, Matthew have said they would like you to come live with them. They live in town and have a school nearby and would give you a good home. But they would have to come out here to get you because you're too young to ride the stage all the way back to Missouri by yourselves.

"Now, Sadie and her mom would like to have you stay here on the ranch with them. You would help Jeremiah and Dustan and Mr. Masengale with the work on the ranch, you know, workin' the cattle and such, and Mary, you'd be helpin' Sadie and her mom around the house here, and on the ranch also.

"And I think Elly would like to have you come with us, but we don't have a home or a ranch or anythin' like that, and we'd be ridin' into the wild country to the west. Now this is a big decision for one so young, and usually you would just be told what to do and you would have to do it, but I think you're both growin' up mighty fast and should have some say in what you do, so what do you think? If it was your choice, where would you like to live?"

Micah visibly shrunk down in his seat, crossing his arms across his chest, and tucking his chin in his collar, glancing at all the faces looking at him, and with a quick glance to Mary he looked back to Reuben. "Do we have to say right now? Can we think about it, maybe talk about it?"

"Of course. It's a big decision. So, tell you what, we," motioning around the table to the many interested adults, "will all go outside, except maybe some of the ladies, and you and Mary can, oh, go for a walk together and talk it over. Then later go to your beds up yonder in the loft, and maybe after a good night's sleep, and gettin' all your questions answered, then things will be a little clearer for you and you can let us know what you think. Would that be alright?"

"Ummhmm," he said, and looked to Mary and motioned for her to come with him as he pushed his chair back from the table and took her hand. They walked out the door and silence fell over the table of adults. Reuben reached for his coffee and brought it to his lips as Sadie asked, "Do you think this Gretchen and Matthew would come out here and get them?" she leaned on the table with her elbows, looking around at the others. "Don't you think they're too young to try to ride the stage all the way to Missouri by themselves?"

Elly answered, "I would not want them riding that far by themselves. Just the ride from Julesburg to Denver was an experience I wouldn't want to relive, and we're adults!"

"It really doesn't make any difference what direction

you go, or how you go, travelin' can be dangerous what with highwaymen, Confederate sympathizers, Indians, and more. Not any place for a couple kids by themselves," declared Jeremiah. "'Sides, we've kinda gotten attached to these little squirts!" He grinned at the thought of the little ones, and the time they spent together.

"If I had a home of my own, I'd sure want to have them with me," said Mabel with a coy smile to Dustan, who squirmed around in his chair a little and ran his finger under his collar that seemed a little tight of a sudden.

"You might have to fight me for 'em," said Sadie, smiling at Mabel and giving a sly look to Jeremiah, who looked around for the coffeepot, wanting his cup refilled.

The adults soon retired to the porch to enjoy the cool of the evening and watch the Creator's show as He painted the western sky from his dazzling palette of colors. The rocking chairs were claimed by the older women, a couple ladderback chairs sufficed for Reuben and Elbert Masengale, and the brothers each claimed a stair for themselves to share with the girls, Sadie, and Mabel. Elly sat down on the plank floor beside Reuben, tucking her feet under her and leaning on his knee.

"So, where'd those two go?" asked Reuben, shading his eyes from the lowering sun.

"Knowin' them two, I'd guess they're in the barn with their horses," declared Jeremiah.

"Sounds reasonable," said Elly, smiling up at Reuben. "What do you think they'll do?"

"Dunno. It's not an easy choice and not one I'd want to make."

Ethel said, "I think it's important for them to have proper schooling and be loved wherever they are!"

"Of course," added Gladys, "but schooling isn't important to a child. Did you see the way Mary's eyes lit up when she remembered the candy in the store?"

"I think you'll be surprised. I believe Micah is older than we think. They've gone through a lot, and he watches out for Mary. I'm trustin' he'll make a right proper decision," resolved Reuben, slipping his arm around Elly's shoulders.

"A boy that age looks at things differently than we do, he'll be thinkin' of the store in town, the candy in the jar, but he'll also be thinkin' about that horse in the barn yonder, and he'll be thinkin' about you two and the adventure of ridin' with you," nodding toward Reuben and Elly. "But I think what will weigh heaviest is havin' a home and a place for his sister," stated Elbert, the oldest of the group, his deep voice resonant with the wisdom of age.

"It'll be getting dark soon, we best fetch them back to get ready for bed," said Sadie, rising and taking Jeremiah's hand as she nodded to the barn. A smile to Mabel and Dustan brought them off the stair and the two couples walked hand in hand to the barn to retrieve the little ones. It was just a moment later that Sadie stood in the door of the barn, motioning to those still on the porch, urging them to come to the barn. The smile on her face told them it was not a problem, but the group hastened their step anyway.

The smiling Sadie, whispering, led them toward the stalls at the back and as they gathered, they saw Micah and Mary, cuddled together on the loose hay below the manger, with the little chestnut mare claimed by Mary and the dapple-grey gelding ridden by Micah, standing stock still on either side as if standing guard over the sleeping little ones. The gelding turned to look at the intruders, and back at the children, and stepped a little closer to the chestnut as if closing ranks to protect their charges.

Reuben and Elly pushed between the horses, stroking their backs, and speaking softly as they moved, and bent down to pick up the siblings, laying their heads on their shoulders and turning back to the ranch house and their pallets in the loft. Elly handed off Mary to Sadie, climbed the ladder to the loft and accepted the girl as Sadie handed her up, then Sadie climbed up to accept Micah. The two girls put the little ones down for the night and quietly slipped down the ladder to rejoin the others on the porch.

"Now that was a sight to warm your heart," declared Mabel, looking at the others and added, "I think they made their choice."

229

I t was not the normal routine for breakfast at the Slade ranch house where Sadie and her mom would fix a big breakfast for the two hired hands, the Cash brothers, and for themselves, but today they had extra guests, their friends, Reuben, and Elly Grundy. Elly had risen early and was helping the ladies fix the big breakfast of biscuits, gravy, flank steaks, fried potatoes, and steaming hot coffee, the aroma of which brought Reuben, sleepy-eyed, from the bed in the guest room. He walked past the table, mumbling a, "Good Mornin'," to the womenfolk and pushed through the door to make his way to the water trough and the pump. With his head under the spigot, he pumped the long handle and cold water cascaded over his rumpled hair, bringing him fully awake. He stood erect, swinging his head side to side to shed some of the water, and fumbled for the flour sack that doubled as a towel.

He ran the towel over his head and neck, looking around in the dim light of early morning to see the thin grey line in the east that foretold the rising sun. Two shadowy figures stumbled from the bunkhouse that

Reuben guessed were the Cash brothers. As they neared the water trough, they grunted to acknowledge Reuben and received a similar greeting in return. Once Jeremiah had doused his head and found the towel, he looked at Reuben who was looking to the east as he ran fingers through his hair, and asked, "Kids up?"

"Nope. But breakfast is about ready," answered Reuben, glancing back at the brothers. With a nod he started back to the house, certain he could smell the fresh coffee even outside. As he pushed open the door, he was surprised to see Mabel and her mother had joined the other ladies in preparing the breakfast.

Reuben also noticed a big skillet of eggs cooking and gave his wife a questioning look. She chuckled and motioned to Mabel and her mother, "They have chickens!"

Reuben grinned, nodding, and reached for a coffee cup to pour himself his morning's necessary potion. He pulled out one of the ladder-back chairs, turned it around and straddled the seat with his arms resting on the crossbar as he watched the ladies finish up the breakfast.

"Ummm, smells good!" came a little voice from the loft. Everyone looked up to see the smiling faces of Micah and Mary, chins resting on the back of their hands, as they lay on their bellies to watch the hubbub of activity. "Flapjacks?"

Mabel's mother smiled. "Just waiting for you so I could get 'em started! But you have to get dressed first!"

Micah jumped to his feet, helped Mary to stand beside him and declared, "We're already dressed!" With a giggle from the loft and laughter from the table, the two youngsters started down the ladder to join everyone at the table. They made the rounds of the ladies, getting hugs and kisses from them all, before seating themselves in their familiar places at the table. Micah's chair held a single flour sack covered feather pillow, and Mary sat atop a big bible but scooted closer to rest her arms on the edge of the big table.

Reuben looked around and turned to Gladys, Mabel's mother, "Are your men joinin' us this mornin'?"

"Oh, I fed them earlier. My husband wanted to get to the upper pasture 'fore the sun came up and the cattle started scattering. He took Bert with him."

Reuben nodded, sipped his coffee, and watched as the ladies put the food on the table. When the table was loaded, Ethel stepped back, hands on hips and asked Reuben, "Would you lead us in prayer, Reuben?"

Reuben nodded, sat his cup down and stood behind the chair and asked the Lord's blessing on the meal and guidance and safety for the day. As he said 'Amen', he heard the voices of both Micah and Mary add their 'Amens' to the rest and he smiled as he turned his chair back around and scooted it closer to the table and sat down. It was a pleasant meal; spirits were high, and the anticipation lay like a blanket over the group who did their best to not ask questions or look at the youngsters more than necessary. But when the table was cleared and the coffee cups refilled, Micah looked at Jeremiah and asked, "So, what are we goin' to do today, Jeremiah? We goin' back to get those strays we left in the south pasture?"

"Uh, I dunno, Micah. I guess that depends on what you two decided to do."

"Oh, we're gonna stay here," he declared very simply. "We talked about it and Mary liked the candy and the way Aunt Gretchen smells, but we like it here better. 'Sides, I ain't cut out to be no store clerk! I'm more of a cowboy, an' Mary doesn't want to leave Sassy!"

"Sassy?" asked Elly.

"She named her horse, Sarsaparilla, but it's too hard to say all the time so she calls her Sassy!"

"What about your family back in Missouri?" asked Mabel, sitting down at the end of the table to listen.

"They're not really family. We just called 'em that cuz of Aunt Margaret, and we only saw 'em a couple times." He looked around at all the faces. "You're more family than they are."

Everyone smiled, the ladies dabbing at their eyes with the corners of their aprons.

Reuben looked at Elly, saw she too was wiping away a few tears, but she looked at Reuben with a smile and a nod as his attention was captured by little Mary asking Elly, "Are you stayin' here too, Elly?"

Elly smiled, scooted closer to little Mary and took her hand in hers and said, "No, Mary. This is not our home, but Sadie, Mabel, and all the others are very good friends, or like Micah said, they're family. So, we will come back and see all of you just as often as we can. Would that be alright?"

"Ummhmm, just don't be too long, alright?" asked Mary, putting her free hand over Elly's and leaning her head closer. Elly smiled, leaning in close and with forehead's touching, assured the girl, "We will come back just as soon and as often as we can!" and embraced Mary in a long hug, kissing her on the cheek as she held her tight.

Elly stood, touched Mary on the cheek and smiled, then looked at Reuben. "I'll finish with our gear in here. You get the horses ready, and I'll be right along." She stepped behind Micah and gave him a big hug, a kiss on the cheek, and whispered in his ear, "We love you!"

Reuben nodded, knowing that Elly did not want to prolong the goodbyes, fearing she would not hold up. It was hard enough leaving the children, but this family had become like her own family, and it would be doubly hard to leave. As she disappeared into the spare room, Reuben looked to Sadie and her mother. "We'll send a telegram to Gretchen and Matthew to let them know about the children. It would be best to let them know they are stayin' with you and give them your address in case they want to send any letters, or such. Would that be alright?"

"Of course. Even though they're not close family, they are what we often called 'back-door' relations and I'm sure they want to know the children will be well loved," answered Ethel, nodding to Sadie who smiled her agreement.

Jeremiah stood, looked at Micah and said, "Well, cowboy. Since you're gonna be workin' on this ranch with the rest of us cowboys, we better go catch up them cayuses and get ready to ride!"

Micah smiled broadly, squirmed off his chair, and called over his shoulder, "Gotta get my hat!" and shinnied up the ladder to the loft. He was proud of his hat and chaps that Mabel had rounded up for him. They had been Mabel's brother's gear and had been stashed in a trunk for some time. When he came down the ladder, it gave all the ladies a touch of melancholy to see the boy so excited and sporting the duds. Mabel's brother and father had fought the Indians alongside Sadie's father when the Cheyenne Dog Soldiers attacked the ranch and captured Sadie and Mabel, and the image of the fight was fresh in the minds of the ladies. But it was a comfort to know Micah would be walking proudly in their footsteps and would hopefully become the man they had proven themselves to be so many times.

Reuben led the horses and the mule from the barn, walking to the hitchrail before the ranch house and saw the ladies and little Mary assembled on the porch. He stood by the rail as Jeremiah, Dustan and Micah led their horses to the rail and the round of goodbyes began. When all were done, and the ladies wiped their tears, Reuben and the Cash brothers shook hands, drew close and slapped each other on the back, and Reuben dropped to one knee before Micah. He took the boy's hand in his and said, "You've shown yourself to be quite a man already, Micah, and I'm countin' on you to be the kind of man that would make your Mom and Dad and me and Elly proud. I know you're goin' to take care of Mary, so..." and he choked up as he stood, still clasping the boy's hand in his.

Micah had doffed his hat to give Elly a big hug and when they parted, Reuben ran his hand through the boy's hair, grinned and drew Elly's appaloosa close. He dropped to one knee, offered his bent knee to Elly and she stepped on it with her right boot, stuffed her left one in the stirrup and swung aboard her spotted mare. Reuben swung into the saddle of Blue and both turned to look at everyone, and with a tip of his hat and a nod of her head, they nudged the horses away from the ranch house, Elly trusting her mare to stay close beside Blue because she could not see where they were going as tears streamed down her cheeks.

The world around them took on a pale pink glow as the rising sun painted the underbellies of the few clouds with the colors of morning. Reuben led them to the nearby river crossing, and they moved from gravel bank to sandbar and across the shallows, to rise from the thickets and willows into the open plains dotted with sage, rabbit brush, and greasewood. They passed a patch of Indian Paintbrush that gave a bright reddish orange splash of color to the dusty tan of the buffalo grass covered prairie.

The rolling hills seemed to ripple before them, random clumps of prickly pear still holding their yellow blossoms, hedgehog cactus opening their bright red blooms, and the cholla with both yellow- and magenta-colored sprouts at the end of their skeletal branches. It was a grand display of God's panorama and Reuben breathed deep of the crisp morning air.

He looked at his woman, her somber expression and glassy stare told of her melancholy thoughts, and he wondered what he could do or say to lift her spirits, when the rattle of trace chains, the squeak of thorough-braces, and the crack of a bullwhip announced the approach of a stagecoach. It came from the east and dragged a dust cloud behind, the shouts of the Jehu and the crack of his whip moved Reuben and Elly from the road to make way.

They looked at the rumbling coach, and both grinned as they recognized the driver and shotgunner as Whiskers and Levi. Both Reuben and Elly stood in their stirrups and lifted their hand to wave and were surprised to see the coach draw to a stop. "Well, lookee here!" declared Levi. "If it ain't two of our favorite people!" He scrambled around and put his foot on the front of the box, the other on the wheel, then the hub and dropped to the ground. He hollered at the passengers, "If'n ya' wanna stretch yore legs, have at it! Only gonna be stopped a minute!" and walked closer to Reuben.

With a glance back at the coach and the passengers getting down, he looked up at Reuben, lowered his voice and said, "Holladay said we was to keep a look out fer you. Said if'n we saw you to make sure you get the message to him 'bout where you are and such. I think he has some kinda special job he wants you to do, you know, involvin' those little badges you keep hidden in yore pocket!" he chuckled as he spoke.

Reuben shook his head, glancing to Elly who had eyebrows raised, and said, "I told him we weren't interested in anymore 'jobs' for him or the governor. But, if he asks, you can tell him the last you saw us we were headed for the mountains!"

Levi chuckled, reached up to shake Reuben's hand, and said, "I'll do it! But in the meantime, you watch yore topknot! Don't wanna see it on no Cheyenne Dog soldier's lance or coup stick!"

Levi hustled the passengers back into the coach, stepped back up to the box and Whiskers shouted, "See ya!" and cracked the whip over the backs of the mules, making them lean into the traces, rocking the stage back on the thoroughbraces, and the dust rose as they pulled away. When the sound subsided, Elly looked at Reuben, "Mountains, huh?"

"Yup. Maybe we can find us a nice place in the trees, lots of green, clear water, game, and more. Then we can build us a cabin and maybe start a family!" he grinned as he spoke.

She giggled, shook her head and said, "We've got a long way to go! I can't even see the mountains from here!" and dug heels to the appaloosa to hasten their journey to the west and the mountains and all they promised.

A CAPTIVATING, VIVID WESTERN CLASSIC – FOR FANS OF THE TRUE WILD WEST.

They had flirted with the distant snowcapped mountains before but never had the opportunity to walk among them. Now with renewed determination, Reuben and his new bride, Elly, set out for those mountains. But the trail they traveled took them through the goldfields of the Pike's Peak Gold Rush of South Park, Colorado Territory.

Evil was running rampant in the outlying areas of the mountain park and when mutilated and disfigured bodies began to litter the landscape from the mountains to the plains, the prospectors and settlers began to let fear rule their lives.

When the supposed killers were finally identified, Reuben joined the posse, not to catch the killers, but to prevent a lawless lynching of possibly innocent travelers. Chosen as a scout to team up with a wily old mountain man, Reuben and his partner would be confronted by a rampaging Ute war party, chase down the bloody killers, and confront those that would take law into their own hands. When blood covered the land, something had to be done, and Reuben could be the man to do it. And all in the middle of God's Country.

AVAILABLE FEBRUARY 2022

ABOUT THE AUTHOR

Born and raised in Colorado into a family of ranchers and cowboys, **B.N. Rundell** is the youngest of seven sons. Juggling bull riding, skiing, and high school, graduation was a launching pad for a hitch in the Army Paratroopers. After the army, he finished his college education in Springfield, MO, and together with his wife and growing family, entered the ministry as a Baptist preacher.

Together, B.N. and Dawn raised four girls that are now married and have made them proud grandparents. With many years as a successful pastor and educator, he retired from the ministry and followed in the footsteps of his entrepreneurial father and started a successful insurance agency, which is now in the hands of his trusted nephew. He has also been a successful audiobook narrator and has recorded many books for several award-winning authors. Now finally realizing his life-long dream, B.N. has turned his efforts to writing a variety of books, from children's picture books and young adult adventure books, to the historical fiction and western genres which are his first love.

CPSIA information can be obtained
at www.ICGtesting.com
Printed in the USA
LVHW030432050122
707889LV00008B/431